YOU CAN'T BRING THAT IN HERE!

and other funny stories

YOU CAN'T BRING THAT IN HERE!

and other funny stories

Collected in partnership with the
Federation of Children's Book Groups

RED FOX

YOU CAN'T BRING THAT IN HERE! and other funny stories
A RED FOX BOOK 0 099 48386 6

First published in Great Britain by Red Fox,
an imprint of Random House Children's Books

This edition published 2005

1 3 5 7 9 10 8 6 4 2

Copyright © Random House Children's Books, 2005
Text copyright © individual authors; see Acknowledgements
Illustrations copyright © Brett Hudson, 2005

Papers used by Random House Children's Books are natural, recyclable
products made from wood grown in sustainable forests. The manufacturing
processes conform to the environmental regulations of the country of origin.

Set in 16/20pt Bembo Schoolbook

Red Fox Books are published by Random House Children's Books,
61–63 Uxbridge Road, London W5 5SA,
a division of The Random House Group Ltd,
in Australia by Random House Australia (Pty) Ltd,
20 Alfred Street, Milsons Point, Sydney, NSW 2061, Australia,
in New Zealand by Random House New Zealand Ltd,
18 Poland Road, Glenfield, Auckland 10, New Zealand,
and in South Africa by Random House (Pty) Ltd,
Endulini, 5A Jubilee Road, Parktown 2193, South Africa

THE RANDOM HOUSE GROUP Limited Reg. No. 954009
www.kidsatrandomhouse.co.uk

A CIP catalogue record for this book is available from the British Library.

Printed and bound in Great Britain by
Cox & Wyman Ltd, Reading, Berkshire

CONTENTS

FOREWORD

The Federation of Children's Book Groups is an amazing organization. For over thirty years it has worked to bring stories to children all over the country. The organization receives no government support. All the work is done by members who receive no payment. They do this voluntary work because they believe children need books.

They know, of course, that reading is an essential educational tool and an important emotional resource for a child's well-being, but experience with books and children has taught them that stories are also wonderful fun! This anthology is dedicated to the sheer enjoyment of stories, which is so much part of the spirit of the Federation.

Sales of this book will help to continue that work and the Federation is grateful to the authors and publishers who donated the stories, and especially to the team at Random House Children's Books who made it all possible.

Some of the authors, like Allan Ahlberg, Robert Swindells and Kaye Umansky, are old friends and supporters of the Federation but all of the authors write very funny stories. Whether you like gorillas, talking pigs, argumentative fairytale characters or UFOs, you'll find them all here. So forget everything solemn – just read and enjoy the stories!

Pat Thomson
Hon. President, Federation of Children's Book Groups

Robert Swindells

YOU CAN'T BRING THAT IN HERE!

Jimmy was absolutely fed up. His mum and dad had gone off to work in America for two years, leaving him to be looked after by his grown-up brother, Osbert. Looked after! That was a laugh, for a start. Osbert had worked in a bakery, but as soon as Mum and Dad started sending money from America, he chucked his job. Nowadays he spent most of his time lying on the sofa in his vest watching telly, slurping beer straight from the can and making rude noises. He neither washed nor shaved nor did anything around the house. The place smelled awful, and the sofa looked like a tatty boat afloat on a sea of can rings, beer cans and screwed-up crisp packets.

Jimmy had to go to school, and when school was over he never had any fun. He couldn't bring his friends home because they were all scared of Osbert, and if there was something good on telly his brother always said, 'Shove off, kid – I'm watching *this*.'

He made Jimmy do all the work – shopping, cooking, cleaning, ironing, gardening – in his spare time. On cold mornings Jimmy had to sit on the lavatory to warm the seat for Osbert, and at bedtime he had to lie in his brother's freezing bed till the sheets were warmed and Osbert came to kick him out. Soon his friends stopped bothering with him, because he couldn't play out or go to football. He grew lonely and sad.

One day on his way home from school, Jimmy found a baby bird which had fallen out of its nest. It was fluffy and cute and Jimmy felt sorry for it. 'It's all right, little bird,' he murmured. 'I'm going to take you home and look after you.'

But when he got home Osbert said, 'You can't bring that in here.'

'Why not?' asked Jimmy, dismayed.

'Birds make a mess,' said Osbert, brushing crumbs off his vest.

'Take it away. Get rid of it.'

Jimmy sniffled as he walked along the street with the nestling cupped in his hands. How could he get rid of it? If he put it down, a cat would get it.

He met an old lady. 'What have you got there?' she asked. Jimmy showed her. 'Oh, the poor wee creature,' she said. 'And are you its new mammy?' Jimmy told the old lady about Osbert and she said, 'I'll tell you what we'll do. I have a beautiful kitten at home. I'll swap you – your bird for my kitten.'

Jimmy was sure Osbert would fall for the kitten, but he didn't. 'You can't bring that in here,' he said.

'Why not?' asked Jimmy.

'Kittens make a mess,' said Osbert, throwing an empty can across the room. 'Get it out.'

Jimmy put the kitten in his pocket and went out. 'Maybe I should take you back to the old lady,' he whispered, but just then a boy from his school came along.

'Hi, Jimmy,' he said. 'What's that in

your pocket?' Jimmy showed him the kitten and told him about Osbert. 'I know,' said the boy. 'I'll take the kitten, and you can have my gerbil.'

'You can't bring that in here,' growled Osbert from the sofa. 'Gerbils throw their food around.'

'But – but . . .' stammered Jimmy.

'No buts!' roared Osbert, chucking half a pork pie at Jimmy's head. 'Get it out of here.'

Jimmy put the gerbil in his pocket and went out. It was getting dark and he was hungry. An old man was coming along the street with a puppy on a lead. 'What's up, son?' he asked, because Jimmy was crying a bit. He told the old man about the gerbil, and about Osbert. 'Well, here,' said the old man. 'Give me your gerbil and take my puppy. Nobody can resist a puppy.'

Osbert could resist a puppy. 'You can't bring that in here,' he snarled. 'Puppies wreck the place.'

'Yes, but . . .' murmured Jimmy.

'No buts!' screamed Osbert, pounding the sofa with his fist till the arm fell off. 'Get it out of here, and when you come back you can get my tea – I'm starving.'

Jimmy was starving too, but he couldn't just abandon the puppy. He trailed along the street holding the lead, wondering what to do. I could try the R.S.P.C.A., he thought. They'd look after him. But when he got to the R.S.P.C.A. it was shut. He was standing, looking at the CLOSED sign and wondering what to do, when a van drew up and a man got out. 'Oh, heck,' the man sighed. 'Closed, and I thought I'd be getting rid of him at last.'

'Who?' asked Jimmy.

'My pet,' growled the man. 'That's who.'

'Why d'you want rid of him?' Jimmy asked.

''Cause he's a gorilla,' said the man.

'A gorilla?' Jimmy was amazed.

The man nodded. 'Aye. Cute and cuddly he was, when he was small, but now . . .' He led Jimmy to the back of the van. 'Look.'

Jimmy peered through the window. Inside the van sat an enormous gorilla.

'Wow!' he gasped. 'What does he eat?'

'Bananas,' said the man. 'Loads and loads of bananas.'

'And where does he sleep?'

'In my bed,' said the man. 'He kicked me out six months ago and now I have to make do with the floor.'

'I'll swap you,' offered Jimmy. 'My puppy for your gorilla.'

The man shook his head. 'You don't want a gorilla, son,' he said.

'Oh yes I do!' cried Jimmy.

Osbert was still on the sofa when Jimmy walked in, his fist buried in the gorilla's giant paw. It was dark in the room and Osbert couldn't see his brother's new pet clearly. 'You can't bring that in here,' he said.

'He isn't bringing me,' rumbled the gorilla. 'I'm bringing *him*. And you can get off that sofa — it's mine.'

Everything's changed at Jimmy's house now. The place sparkles, which isn't surprising because Osbert never stops cleaning it. He daren't stop, because Bozo the gorilla likes a tidy house, and Bozo usually gets what he wants. When Osbert isn't lugging great bagfuls of bananas from the supermarket he's sweeping, polishing, dusting and hoovering.

Jimmy's friends drop in all the time to watch TV, play video games and see Bozo. Until recently Osbert had a girlfriend, but she's left him now. She didn't like it when Osbert brought her home one evening and Bozo said, 'You can't bring that in here.'

Allan Ahlberg

TOO MANY BEARS

One evening a little girl named Dinah
Price kissed her mum and dad
goodnight, climbed the stairs, went
into her room – and found three bears
in her bed. These bears were a father
bear, a mother bear and a baby bear.

They were lying side by side, with the baby bear in the middle. They appeared to be sleeping.

Dinah Price knew a bit about bears. When she was an even littler girl, her mum used to tell her a story about some bears and the trouble they had had with another little girl named Goldilocks. So Dinah went up to the bed with the bears in it and said, 'Who's this sleeping in *my* bed?'

Straight away the bears opened their eyes and shouted, 'Us!' And they laughed – all three of them. They were only pretending to be asleep.

Dinah Price stood at the foot of the bed and looked at the bears. The evening sunlight was shining into the room. Through the open window came the sound of a lawn-mower. The next-door neighbour was cutting his grass.

The bears lay in the bed and looked at Dinah Price. From time to time they gave each other a little nudge and smiled. They did not seem embarrassed to be in someone else's bed. They showed no sign of leaving.

'What are you doing here?' said Dinah.

'Resting,' said the father bear.

'But how did you get in?'

'That would be telling. Maybe we climbed up the drainpipe.'

'Or down the chimney,' said the mother bear.

'Like Santa Claus!' the baby bear said.

'There isn't a chimney,' said Dinah. 'We've got central heating.'

At that moment through the open window came the chimes of an ice cream van. The baby bear's little eyes lit up. 'Can we go home now?'

'No,' said the mother bear. 'We've only just got here.' Then, in a whisper to Dinah, she added, 'Take no notice. What he really wants is an ice cream.'

'What are you whispering about?' said the baby bear. And he said, 'Can I have an ice cream?'

'Wait and see,' said the mother bear.

Dinah Price thought for a minute. She would not have minded an ice cream herself. She said, 'But shouldn't you be going home anyway? It's bedtime!'

'That's no problem,' said father bear. 'We're in bed.'

'Yes, but it's not yours – it's mine. And I have to go to sleep. I will get into trouble if I don't.'

'That's too bad,' said father bear. 'We like it here.'

'It's comfy,' the mother bear said.

The baby bear knelt up in the bed

and whispered in his mother's ear. For the first time Dinah noticed he had her woolly duck in the bed with him. He must have taken it from the toy box.

The mother bear nodded and smiled. Then the baby bear turned to Dinah. 'My mum says you could tell us a story!'

'A story?' Dinah frowned. 'You want *me* to tell *you* a story?'

'That's the idea,' said the mother bear.

Dinah Price thought for a minute. 'If I did tell you a story, would you promise to go home then – to your own beds?'

For a moment there was silence. The bears looked at each other. The baby bear whispered in his mother's ear again, and then his father's. After that all three of them spoke at once:

'Yes!'

'That's fair enough!'

'It's a promise!'

So Dinah Price pulled up her stool, picked up a book from her bedside table and began to read. Well, the truth is, she pretended to read, for she was making the story up. 'Once upon a time there were three bears—'

'Heard it already!' said the baby bear.

'No, you haven't,' said Dinah. 'This is a different one. Listen!'

And this is the story she told.

'Once upon a time there were three bears who lived together in a house of their own in a wood. One of them was a little, small, wee bear—'

'That's me!' the baby bear said.

'One was a middle-sized bear, and the other was a great, huge bear. One day these bears were out walking.

They came to a neat little house on the edge of the wood. It had a red roof, yellow curtains and roses round the door. It was a girl named Goldilocks's house.'

'She's a little madam, that one,' the mother bear said.

'Well, the bears came up to the house and peeped through the window. Goldilocks was out. She had gone to play and have tea at her friend's house. So the bears opened the door and went in. They went down the hall and into the kitchen. There on the table was a delicious bowl of, er . . . pineapple jelly, which Goldilocks was saving for her tea.'

'You said she was having tea at her friend's house,' the father bear said.

'Well, supper then. Anyway, there was the jelly. So first the great, huge bear tasted it, but it was too sweet for him. Then the middle-sized bear tasted it, but it was too . . . wobbly.'

'I like it wobbly,' said the mother bear.

'Then the little, small, wee bear tasted the jelly and for him it was neither too sweet nor too wobbly, but just right. So he ate it all up.'

'Lovely!' The baby bear clapped his little paws. 'I want a drink of water.'

'No, you don't,' said the father bear. 'You have just had all that jelly.'

'And never even gave your poor old mother a lick of the spoon,' the mother bear said.

'Next the bears went upstairs to Goldilocks's bedroom. By this time all three of them were feeling tired from their walk; also, they were quite cheeky bears, as you can see. So they got into the bed and went to sleep. Then – this is the exciting part – then, Goldilocks came back!'

'From her friend's house,' the father bear said.

'That's it. Well, when Goldilocks saw the front door open, she said, "Wow – somebody has been at my front door and left it open." When she saw the empty bowl on the kitchen table, she said, "Wow – somebody has been at my pineapple jelly and eaten it all up." '

'Ha, ha!' said the baby bear.

'When she went upstairs and saw the bears in her bed, she said, "Wow – somebody has been sleeping in my bed – and they're still in it!" '

'Serves her right,' the father bear said.

And the baby bear said, 'Then what

did she do?'

'She thought for a minute,' said Dinah, who was herself thinking for a minute. 'She thought for a minute and said, "Who's this sleeping in *my* bed?" And the bears woke up then, and they said, "Us!"'

'Weren't they only pretending to be asleep?' said the baby bear.

'No, they were really asleep. So then Goldilocks gave the three bears a good talking to. She said they had no business being in her house, eating her pineapple jelly and sleeping in her bed.'

'She's got a nerve,' said the mother bear.

'Then the bears promised to leave if only Goldilocks would tell them a story; so she did. She told them a story and they listened and said thank-you-very-much. After that they went home

– because a promise is a promise –
they went home and—'

'Wait a minute,' the baby bear said.
'What was the story *she* told?'

'I don't remember. Anyway, that's
another story!'

'I bet I know what it was,' said the
mother bear. She began to smile. 'I bet
it was like this: Goldilocks said, "Once
upon a time there were three bears".
Then the little, small, wee bear said he
had heard it already—'

'I have heard it already *already*!' said
the baby bear.

And the father bear said, 'My head
is spinning. How many bears have we
got now?'

' "Then the three bears went out for
a walk",' said the mother bear, ' "and
came to Goldilocks's house and went
inside and ate her pineapple jelly." '

'Only the little, small, wee bear ate

the jelly,' said the baby bear.

'No – they all ate it this time,' said the mother bear. 'In fact, come to think of it, the middle-sized bear ate most of it. Well, they ate the jelly and went upstairs for a lie-down, and Goldilocks came back and found them there and—'

'Told them to clear off out of it!' said Dinah, who was getting impatient.

'No, she didn't,' said the baby bear.

'Yes, she did. She said, "You bears get out of here or I will fetch my daddy, who is a hunter."'

'A hunter?' the baby bear looked puzzled. 'What's a hunter?'

'Don't answer that,' whispered the mother bear. 'We haven't told him about hunters yet. He's too young.'

'What are you whispering about?' said the baby bear. And he said,

22

'What's a hunter?'

'A man,' the mother said. 'A man who cuts the trees down.'

'That's a wood-cutter!'

The mother bear turned to Dinah. 'Go on with the story.'

'Right,' said Dinah. 'So anyway, Goldilocks told the three bears about her daddy and his gun, and that was enough for them.'

'What's a gun?' said the baby bear.

'Don't answer *that*,' the mother bear said.

'That was enough for them,' said Dinah. 'They wasted no time, but jumped out of the bed, out of the window and ran off through the woods to their own house, their own pineapple jelly – and *their own* beds! The End.'

At this point Dinah slammed the book shut, startling the father bear, who had been dozing off. The mother bear sat up in the bed. 'That wasn't a bad story.' She yawned and stretched. 'Except for the last bit.'

Dinah Price stood up and put the book on her bedside table. It was darker in the room now. A smell of cut grass was coming through the open window. The noise of the mower had stopped. In a tree outside the window, birds were twittering. Downstairs the phone began to ring.

'Was Goldilocks's father really a "you-know-what"?' the mother bear said.

'What's a you-know-what?' said the baby bear.

'Yes, he was.' Dinah could feel her feet getting cold inside her slippers. 'He was a terror.' And she said, 'Are you going home now?'

'Certainly,' said the mother bear.

And the father bear said, 'We can take a hint.'

The three bears clambered out of the bed. The father bear and the mother bear tidied the bedclothes and plumped up the pillow.

'Do you have far to go?' said Dinah.

'That would be telling,' said the mother bear. 'It could be miles and miles!'

'Or just down the road,' the father bear said.

Then Dinah spotted the baby bear. He was trying to sneak off with her woolly duck. Luckily, the mother bear spotted him too. She made him give it back.

After that the three bears climbed out onto the window ledge, said goodbye to Dinah Price, went down the drainpipe and across the grass, waved goodbye to Dinah – who was watching them go – and disappeared into the rhododendron bushes at the far end of the garden.

The last words Dinah heard was the baby bear halfway down the drainpipe saying, 'Can we have pineapple jelly when we get home?' And his mother's reply: 'Wait and see.'

Dinah Price shut the window and pulled the curtains across. She said to herself, 'I will tell my friend about this tomorrow.' After that she got into the bed – still warm from the bears – and slept till morning.

Mick Gowar

THE AMAZING
TALKING PIG

It was a cold autumn night on
Brown's Farm. Mr Brown, the farmer,
had finished washing up his supper
things, and was just settling down
in his comfy armchair to read his
library book, when there was a gentle
Tap-tappity-tap on the front door.

'Bother!' muttered Mr Brown,
grumpily. 'I was just getting
comfortable.'

He looked at the clock on the
mantelpiece: it was half-past nine.
'Who can that be, so late?' he
wondered.

Cautiously, Mr Brown opened the door and looked out. There was no one there. He was just closing the door when he heard a cough. Mr Brown peered out into the darkened farmyard; there was still no one there. He started to close the door again.

'Ah-hem, ah-*hem*!' said a voice.

It seemed to be coming from the step. Mr Brown looked down and saw, to his astonishment, a small pink pig.

'Hullo,' said the pig, politely.

'WAAAH!' yelled Mr Brown, staggering back.

'I said: Hullo,' repeated the pig.

'You . . . you . . . you . . . can . . .' spluttered Mr Brown.

'. . . come in?' suggested the pig. 'Thanks very much. I will.'

And it walked past Mr Brown and into the warm cosy sitting room.

'Wow!' exclaimed the pig, looking

round the room. 'This is some sty!' It sniffed the carpet. 'And *that* is what I call High Class Straw!'

Mr Brown tottered unsteadily into the room.

'But . . . but . . . but,' he gasped, 'you can . . . can . . .'

'. . . sit down and make myself at home?' suggested the pig. 'Ta, very much!'

With a quick spring it jumped into Mr Brown's armchair.

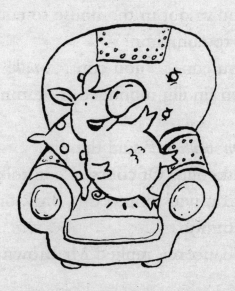

'*Very* nice!' said the pig, snuggling down into the cushions. 'And what's this?'

It sniffed Mr Brown's library book, which he'd left open on the chair. 'Oooh! I see I'm just in time for a snack,' said the pig, licking its lips. 'Goody!' And it tore out a page and began chewing.

'Not bad,' said the pig thoughtfully, as it swallowed the page. 'I prefer a little warm swill, myself, but if this is all you've got in the house to eat, who am I to complain?'

'You can . . . you can . . . *talk*!' Mr Brown finally managed to stammer out.

'*Oh, brilliant!*' said the pig sarcastically. 'Of course I can talk, what do you think I am, thick or something?'

'No, no, no,' replied Mr Brown

hastily. 'It's just that . . . well . . . but
. . . but you've never spoken to *me*
before.'

'Haven't needed to,' explained the
pig. 'Everything was OK until now.
Nice food, clean straw, cosy sty, good
conversation with the other pigs –
what more could a pig want? But
tonight? *Brrrr!* That sty is *not* the place
to spend a cold night, I can tell you.
Talk about freezing? I was colder than
a penguin's bottom!

'So I said to myself: *Horatio* – that's
my name, by the way – *Horatio*, I said,
*this is the time of year when a pig needs a
warm fire, a cup of hot cocoa, and a proper
bed with plenty of warm blankets*. So here
I am.'

Mr Brown shook his head in
amazement.

The pig suddenly looked worried.
'You do *have* cocoa, don't you?' it asked.

'Er . . . yes . . .' replied Mr Brown.

'Great!' said the pig. 'I like two sugars. Oh, and don't let the milk boil. I can't *stand* skin on my cocoa.'

Mr Brown walked out to the kitchen like a robot in shock. He opened the fridge and, as if in a dream, he poured a pint of milk into a saucepan and put it on the hotplate.

As he waited for the milk to heat, Mr Brown tried to get used to the idea of his amazing guest.

'Fantastic!' he said to himself. 'Unbelievable! A talking pig! I've never heard of anything like it before. I'm sure it must be the only talking pig in the whole world . . .'

'Yoo-hoo! Mr Brown!' called the pig from the sitting room. 'Don't forget what I said: no skin on my cocoa, please.'

Mr Brown poured the cocoa into

two cups – one for him, one for the pig. Then he had second thoughts, and poured the pig's cocoa into a bigger cup. Then he had third thoughts, and poured a large whisky into his cocoa. (He'd had a nasty shock; he needed a little something.)

The only one in the whole world . . . thought Mr Brown, as the whisky glugged into his cup. This could make me famous! I can see the headlines in all the papers: FARMER BROWN AND HIS AMAZING TALKING PIG! I'll be on radio and TV, too! That pig could make me rich! That pig could make me a millionaire! I'd better be very nice to that pig.

'Here you are,' said Mr Brown, putting the pig's cocoa down in front of the fire. 'And if you want anything else, anything at all – just tell me . . .' By midnight, Mr Brown bitterly regretted his promise to give the pig anything it wanted. There seemed to be nothing that the pig *didn't* want. Mr Brown had never had to work so hard in all his life.

First, the pig had wanted a second cup of cocoa. Then the pig had asked for a snack.

'A *proper* one this time, please!'

So Mr Brown had made up a special warm mash to the pig's favourite recipe. The pig had sat in the armchair yelling out orders, while Mr Brown scurried frantically in the kitchen.

'Two jars of strawberry jam – large ones – and one tin of treacle. Now, crumble in sixteen Weetabix – got that?'

'Er, yes . . .' Mr Brown had replied, desperately crumbling Weetabix as fast as he could.

'Now mix up four pounds of creamed potatoes – fresh, mind, none of that powdered rubbish – and use *real* butter. Humans may not be able to tell the difference between margarine and butter, but pigs can! And when you've creamed the potatoes, add two jars of marmalade – the expensive sort, with big chunks of orange peel. Then two jars of Marmite, three pounds of stewed prunes. And finally, two tablespoons of Double Strength Madras Curry Powder – for that extra tingle, know what I mean?'

After its meal, the pig demanded a bubble bath, in the old tin tub in front of the fire.

'I can't stand cold bathrooms,' the pig had explained.

Poor Mr Brown. He'd had to run between the kitchen and the sitting

room with pots and pans and kettles of hot water. Then he'd had to mix up a bubble bath using two giant containers of washing-up liquid and a bottle of very expensive aftershave his sister Lydia had given him for his birthday.

Mr Brown was now weak with tiredness. The pig wasn't.

'Let's have some music,' said the pig. 'I see you've got a banjo. Let's have a sing–song!'

So Mr Brown played the banjo until his fingertips were sore and throbbing, while the pig sang every song that Mr Brown knew in the most awful squealing tenor voice that Mr Brown had ever heard. The pig also changed all the words so that all the songs were about pigs. Its favourite songs were: 'Old MacDonald Had A Pig' and 'All Pigs Bright And Beautiful'.

'I'm beginning to feel a little sleepy,' said the pig, when it had finished singing.

Mr Brown breathed a huge sigh of relief.

'So, time for a bedtime story – or two!' announced the pig.

Bleary-eyed and sore-throated, Mr Brown stumbled through *The Three Little Pigs* and *The Three Billy Goats Gruff* – but with the goats changed to pigs, of course.

'Well,' said the pig, eventually, 'time for bed – I mustn't miss my beauty sleep. Where's my room?'

Mr Brown led the way upstairs, and into the guest bedroom.

'Oh, dear,' said the pig, inspecting the bed. 'Tut-tut! This is no good – the bed's too narrow, and the mattress is much too lumpy. I'll have to sleep in your bed.'

Wearily, Mr Brown led the way to his own room.

'Not bad,' said the pig, snuggling under the covers. 'But still not perfect.'

'What's the matter *now*?' groaned Mr Brown.

'No hotty-totty,' replied the pig.

'No *what*?' asked Mr Brown.

'No hot-water bottle,' said the pig. 'You don't want me to catch cold, do you?'

Mr Brown staggered downstairs to fetch the hot-water bottle.

'And I forgot, I'll need a drink of water, too,' the pig said as Mr Brown came back into the room.

With a weary groan Mr Brown fetched a bowl of water.

'Now a good-night kiss . . .' said the pig, puckering its snout.

'Do I have to?' asked Mr Brown.

'Yes,' said the pig, 'you do!'

Mr Brown woke up. He was still in his armchair. The fire was out, and the morning light was glinting through a thin crack between his curtains. His library book had fallen face down on the floor at his feet. He looked at the clock on the mantelpiece: it was half-past seven.

The pig!

Mr Brown sat up, horrified. Then he chuckled to himself. It had all been a dream. He must have fallen asleep in his chair and dreamt the whole thing!

Mr Brown got to his feet and stretched. Then he bent down and began to rake out the cold ashes of his fire.

'WAAAAH!' yelled Mr Brown, as something wet and snout-like tapped him on the back of the neck.

'Good morning!' said the cheerful,

snuffly voice behind him. 'What's for breakfast? I'm ravenous!'

BOB AND THE HOUSE ELVES

Bob the Builder was a very happy man. He lived alone in a little messy house that suited him just fine. He looked after himself quite well. He swept the floor on the first of the month, and made his bed on Sundays. He always meant to clean the bath, but it never seemed to need it. Most nights he ate baked beans out of a tin, and watched TV. On Saturday mornings he did his shopping. On Saturday nights his mates came round for a game of cards, and they all ordered takeaway pizza.

One Thursday morning, Bob woke up and went downstairs as usual. He knew at once that something was wrong. Someone had cleaned his kitchen. Nothing looked the same. Even the kettle. Someone had washed the windows. He could see straight through. He could see his garden, and the sun, and his new neighbour, Lily Sweet, hanging out her clothes. And on the table, instead of the Cornflakes box, was a dainty plate of fairy bread and a flower in a vase.

'What's this?' said Bob, amazed. He sat down at the table, and ate some fairy bread to settle his nerves. And then he got an awful fright. Three tiny creatures skittered from behind the fridge. Next minute, they were holding hands, and dancing in a ring.

'Crikey!' said Bob. 'So that's it! I got elves!'

He scratched his bristly chin. 'Scat!' he roared, and waved his arms.

The elves giggled. It was a twittering, twinkling sound that sent shivers up Bob's spine. He rolled up his paper and whacked!

But he missed.

The next day, when Bob woke up, his hair was a mass of fairy knots. The whole house was horribly clean and bright. There were flower petals in the bath, and fairy dust in the Cornflakes. And elves were everywhere.

'Crikey, this is awful!' groaned Bob.

But things got worse and worse.

The elves had cleaned his working boots. They'd washed his blue singlet, mended his shorts, and polished his hard hat. He had to go to work all clean. His mates just laughed and laughed.

There was a fairy cake in his lunch box, and fairy bread as well. He had to eat them. He was hungry. His mates laughed even more.

Bob stomped into his house that night determined to clean out all the elves.

But while he'd been away, things had got out of hand.

'Crikey! It's a plague,' he said.

Tomorrow night, his mates were coming round for cards. He had to get rid of the elves by then. But how?

He tried loud music.

He tried throwing things.

He set traps.

He stood and shouted at the top of his voice.

But nothing worked.

Bob knew he needed help. He ate some fairy bread to settle his nerves. And then he had a bright idea.

'I can't be the only bloke with elves,' he said. 'There must be some sort of cure.'

On Saturday morning, Bob went to the chemist shop. It was crowded.

'Can I help you, sir?' said a lady in a pale pink smock.

Bob went red. He felt embarrassed to admit his problem. But he knew he had to do it.

He leant across the counter. 'I got a bit of an elf problem,' he said, in a low, low voice.

'What sort of health problem do you have?' asked the lady in the pale pink smock. 'Come on, don't be shy.'

'Not health. Elf,' said Bob, going even redder. 'I got elves, at home.'

'Oh *elves*,' said the lady in the pale pink smock, standing back and looking down her nose. She turned and shouted to her friend along the counter. 'Hey, Leanne! This man's got elves. We got anything for that?'

The other customers looked at Bob. They said 'tut-tut' and edged away, or shook their heads, and smiled.

'You sure it's elves?' Leanne yelled back. 'Not pixies, are they? Gnomes, or sprites? Not fairies, dwarves or leprechauns?'

'He said elves,' bellowed the lady in the pale pink smock.

Bob wished that he could disappear. 'Crikey,' he muttered. 'Give me a break!'

'I'm sorry, sir, we're out of "Elf-Rid" at the moment,' called Leanne. 'There'll be more in on Tuesday.'

'Tuesday's much too late,' groaned Bob, and crept away.

At home, Bob ate some fairy bread to settle his nerves. Then he had a bright idea. He looked up Pest Exterminators in the phone book and started ringing up. Most of the numbers didn't answer, but finally one did.

'Pesky Pest Control. Name your poison,' said a cheerful man. It was a relief to hear a friendly voice.

'Will you do a job on elves?' Bob said, in a low, low voice.

'Of course we'd do the job ourselves. Who else? There's only me and my brother here. What's biting you, mate?' Mr Pesky replied.

Bob felt himself go red again. 'Not

selves. Elves,' he said. 'Me house is crawling with elves. I'm desperate.'

'Oh, *elves*,' exclaimed Mr Pesky. 'Right, then, I'm your man. You're sure it's elves you've got? Not pixies, maybe? Gnomes, or sprites? Not fairies, dwarves or leprechauns?'

'Crikey, I don't know,' cried Bob. 'What's the difference?'

'Oh, there's all the difference in the world, mate,' Mr Pesky said.

Bob thought a bit. 'Well, mine are little, they've got small wings, they dance around a lot and they like to clean up stuff.'

'Yep. Sounds like elves all right. Or fairies,' Mr Pesky said. 'Pixies go in more for causing trouble.'

'Mine cause trouble,' said Bob gloomily. 'Crikey, you got no idea.'

Mr Pesky sighed. 'Might be a new breed, mate,' he said. I'd better come and take a look. I can fit you in Wednesday week.'

'Next Wednesday week?' roared Bob. 'I can't wait that long. I'm going bonkers! Can't you come today?'

'No way,' said Mr Pesky. 'I'm up to my eyeballs here, mate. Booked up solid. It's Wednesday week or nothing.'

'Make it nothing, then!' growled Bob. 'Mate!' He slammed down the phone. He wasn't usually so rude, but he was quite upset.

Bob ate some fairy bread to settle his nerves. Then he had a bright idea.

'I know,' he said. 'I'll get a book. There's books on everything these days. There must be one to deal with this.'

So he went down

50

to the library. He'd never been in it before. There were thousands of books all round the walls. He didn't know where to start. He knew he'd have to ask.

Behind the counter was a lady in a bright green dress. She turned around and saw him.

'Hello, Bob,' she said. 'What can I do for you?'

It was Lily Sweet, the lady who'd just moved in next door.

Bob went very, very red. He felt like running. But he knew he had to go through with this. The situation was desperate.

He leant across the counter. 'You got any books on elves?' he asked, in a low, low voice.

'Oh, yes. We have lots of books on the shelves,' Lily said. 'What sort of book did you want?'

'Not shelves, *elves*,' said Bob, going even redder. 'Have you got any books on elves?'

'Oh, *elves*,' said Lily Sweet. But she smiled, and she didn't shout. 'And is it just elves you want? Not pixies, or sprites, for example? Not fairies or gnomes or leprechauns?'

'I don't think so,' said Bob. 'I think it's elves, all right. Unless it's fairies. Or pixies. Could be a new breed, I reckon.'

Lily smiled. She had kind grey eyes. 'Let's see what we can find,' she said. She went away for a moment, and came back with a big thick book. It had a brightly coloured picture of elves, fairies and pixies on the front.

She stamped the card at the back and gave the book to Bob. 'You can keep it till next week,' she said.

'Next week will be too late,' said Bob. 'I've only got till seven tonight.'

He thanked Lily, left the library and crept off home, trying to hide the book under his coat. It was the most embarrassing walk of his life.

When Bob got home, the elves were worse. He ate some fairy bread to settle his nerves. Then he had a bright idea. He pitched his tent in the living room and zipped himself inside. Then he read the book in peace, all afternoon.

At five past six he yelled '*Bingo!*' He'd found what he was looking for. There it was, in black and white, on page 117.

'Sounds simple enough,' said Bob.

He rushed into the kitchen with the book. He got a saucepan ready. He started to assemble the ingredients.

A Recipe Guaranteed to Banish Elves from Houses, Boats and Caravans

Tomato sauce
A cube of ice
A slice of mouldy cheese
3 snips of dirty fingernail
And 22 baked beans

Stir it well and heat it up
Then give the pan a whack.
And say these words
While turning round
With your head inside a sack:
'Elven folk!
I have spoke!
Begone, and don't come back!'

Tomato sauce, ice, mouldy cheese, dirty fingernails – no problem. But when it came to baked beans . . .

'Crikey!' howled Bob. 'I'm all out.'

He'd been so upset that he'd forgotten to do his Saturday morning shopping.

He grabbed his wallet and ran outside. But when he got to the corner shop, it was shut.

'Open up!' he yelled, and beat on the door with his fists. But there was no one there. Tony, who owned the shop, had left long ago. After all, it was Saturday night, and he was going to the movies with his girlfriend.

Bob trailed home in despair. 'Twenty-two baked beans,' he muttered, as he walked. 'That's all I wanted. A few miserable baked beans. Was that too much to ask?'

Back in his house, Bob ate some

fairy bread to settle his nerves.

And then he thought of his neighbour, Lily Sweet. Did ladies like her
ever eat baked beans? he wondered.

It was worth a try.

Bob went next door and knocked. Lily
answered the door. When she saw him,
she smiled.

'Well, hello, Bob,' she said. 'What
can I do for you?'

Bob went red. 'I was just
wondering,' he mumbled, 'if you'd have
any baked beans at all?'

'Oh, dear. I'm very sorry, but I
don't,' said Lily Sweet. 'I ate the very
last of mine for dinner, just now. If only
you'd come in two minutes earlier . . .'

'Oh, no!' groaned Bob, and clutched
his head.

'Do you need baked beans
especially?' she asked. 'I have kidney

beans. I have haricot beans, and broad beans and butter beans. I have green beans, string beans, jumping beans and jelly beans. Would any of those do instead?'

'I don't reckon they would,' said Bob. 'It's a recipe, see. Tomato sauce, a cube of ice, a slice of mouldy cheese, three bits of dirty fingernail – and twenty-two baked beans.'

A strange expression appeared on Lily's face. 'But – isn't that the recipe for getting rid of elves?' she asked. 'From houses, boats and caravans?'

Bob went even redder, and hung his head. 'Yeah,' he confessed. 'It was in that book I got from the library.'

Lily clasped her hands. 'So – do you have elves, Bob? In your house? Now?'

Bob knew he couldn't lie to Lily. She had such nice, kind grey eyes.

'Yeah,' he muttered. 'A whole mob

of 'em. They've been driving me bonkers. And I can't get rid of 'em, Lily. Crikey, I've tried everything.'

He looked up, to see how she was taking it. She looked very, very shocked. 'Oh, Bob,' she breathed. 'I'm so sorry.'

Bob went the reddest he'd ever been. And he was, to tell the truth, a bit disappointed. He'd thought that Lily might have tried to make him feel better, instead of worse.

'Oh, well, I s'pose it could happen to anyone,' he said bravely. 'See you around, then. Bye.' He turned to go back to his house.

'No!' Lily cried. 'Don't go. You don't understand. Oh, Bob, this is all my fault!'

'*Your* fault?' Bob said. He was astounded.

'Oh, yes,' said Lily, very upset. 'I had elves at my last house, and they must have moved with me, in my furniture. They're like that, you know. Once you've got them, they tend to stay.'

'Don't I know it!' said Bob, with feeling.

Lily shook her head. 'But I had no idea they'd spread next door, into your place,' she said. 'They must have found a hole, or something. And all this time they've been worrying you. I feel terrible.'

She looked so unhappy that Bob patted her arm. 'Don't you give it another thought, Lil,' he said, trying to sound cheerful. 'Look, how about you give me some kidney beans. I'll have a go with them.'

'Oh, Bob, if only I'd known why you wanted that book!' cried Lily. 'I could have told you – that old recipe doesn't work! Even with proper baked beans. I know. I tried it when I first got elves years and years ago while I was on holiday.'

'What!?' yelled Bob. 'Doesn't work?' He went very, very red. This time, it wasn't because he was embarrassed. It was because he was furious.

'You mean I read that book in a tent for the whole rotten afternoon for nothing?' he shouted. 'You mean whoever wrote that book's a con man? A crook?' He clenched his fists, and looked around in a rage. 'Where's he hang out? I'll soon show him what's what. The low, miserable . . .'

He wasn't usually violent, but he was quite upset.

'No, no,' said Lily quickly, patting Bob's arm. 'I'm sure the recipe *used* to work, a long time ago, Bob. But elves have got used to it, that's the trouble. These days it doesn't scare them at all.'

'Is that right?' said Bob, staring.

Lily nodded. 'Actually, mine quite like the mixture. On toast,' she said. 'And they've learned the words of the curse off by heart. They've made them into a song. They often sing it to put their babies to sleep at night. It sounds quite sweet, really.'

Bob the Builder was a brave man, but he knew when he was beaten.

'Then I've had it, Lil,' he said. 'I've shot me bolt. I've come to the end of the line. I'm up the creek without a paddle. In half an hour me mates are coming round for cards. They see those elves, and I'll never live it down. Oh, well.' He straightened his shoulders. 'That's life.'

Lily looked confused. 'But − if your

friends are the problem, why don't you just ask your elves to keep out of the way, for a while?' she said.

'*Ask* them?' Bob was astounded, all over again. 'Crikey, I've asked them to get out of it a million times, mate. I've shouted and yelled till I'm blue in the face!'

'But shouting won't do any good!' exclaimed Lily. 'Elves never listen when you shout. It just makes them over-excited and troublesome. You have to speak softly and politely to them. Or better still, write them a note. They love notes.'

'I'm not much of a one for writing notes,' Bob mumbled, going red all over again.

'I'll help you, then,' Lily said.

So Lily and Bob went into his house, and she helped him to write the note.

The note said:

Dear Elves,
Would you be so kind as to leave this house
from 10 minutes to 7 this evening until 2am?
I am expecting guests.
Thank you very much.
With best wishes,

Yours sincerely,

Bob (the Builder)

They put the note on the fridge,
where all the elves could see it. And
five minutes later there wasn't an elf in
sight.

'It's like magic,' said Bob.

'It's just polite,' said Lily. 'Well, I'd
better be going. Your friends will be
coming any minute.'

Bob took her to the door.

'Tomorrow, could you help me write a note to tell them to go away for good?' he asked hopefully. 'The elves, I mean.'

Lily looked doubtful. 'I could, I suppose. But are you sure you really want that, Bob? I know they're a bit of a nuisance sometimes, but I quite like having them around the place myself. They do all the housework for a start. They mend my clothes. And I find the fairy bread gives me bright ideas.'

Bob frowned in thought. 'Crikey, you might have a point there, Lil,' he said at last. 'I have had a few bright ideas, lately. And I'd be just as happy never to pick up a broom again, I can tell you that. Housework's a pain in the neck.'

'I agree,' said Lily. 'So what do you

want to do?'

But Bob didn't quite know. Now he had another problem. He wanted the elves to go. But he wanted them to stay, as well.

Bob's mates all arrived after that, so Bob and Lily couldn't talk any more. But after his mates went home, Bob thought about his problem quite a lot. He thought about it so much that he couldn't sleep.

At two a.m. the elves came back. They cleaned up all the empty glasses and pizza boxes. Then they swept the floor and washed up, and put a plate of fairy bread on the table.

Bob made himself a cup of tea, sat down at the table and ate some fairy bread to settle his nerves.

Then he had a bright idea. Without even waiting for Lily Sweet, he got paper and a pen and wrote the elves a note.

Dear Elves,

Thanks for all your work, and the fairy bread.
I really appreciate it. But if you want to stay in
my house, please note the following Rules:

1. Please don't clean my working boots.
2. Please don't polish my hard hat.
3. Please don't tie my hair in knots at night.
4. Please don't make the house too tidy. It
makes me nervous.
5. Please note that I like Vegemite sandwiches
for lunch.
Or tuna sandwiches. Or cheese. Or peanut
butter.
Not fairy bread (or cakes).
6. Please leave the house between 7 o'clock
and 2am on Saturday nights because I always
have guests then.

Thank you very much.

With best wishes,

Yours sincerely,

Bob (the Builder)

Bob put the note on the fridge, and went to bed.

And after that, there was no more trouble.

Now that Bob wasn't shouting at them, the elves became quiet and very easy to live with. Sometimes, they were so quiet that Bob didn't even know they were there – except that his house was always clean and tidy (but not *too* tidy), and none of his clothes had holes in them any more.

The elves obeyed all the rules Bob had written for them that night, so his mates had no more reason to laugh at him. And the Saturday card nights were always a great success. Bob's mates quite liked the house being a bit tidier. It was easier to find somewhere to sit, they said.

And of course, Bob and Lily Sweet

saw a lot of one another. After all, they had plenty in common. Elves and baked beans and not liking housework, for a start.

They always had lunch together on Sundays. Sometimes they'd have it in Bob's house, sometimes in Lily's. Then they'd go for a walk in the park, while the elves cleaned up.

Bob wasn't much of a one for talking about his feelings, but after lunch one Sunday he knew the time had come. He'd worked out just what he was going to say. He ate a last piece of fairy bread to settle his nerves. Then he took Lily's hand across the table.

'Lil,' he said in a low, low voice. 'You're a special lady. No elf could take your place.'

Lily went red. 'No wealth could take your place, either, Bob,' she whispered. 'Who cares about money, anyway?'

Bob felt very, very happy. 'How about we get hitched, then?' he said.

And Lily said that was the brightest idea he'd ever had.

So they got married, and Bob made their two little houses into one big one for them to share. The elves were very pleased. The renovations made a lot of mess, so they had plenty of work to do.

And besides, being elves, there was nothing they liked better than a story with a happy ending.

Terry Jones

THE STAR OF
THE FARMYARD

There was once a dog who could perform the most amazing tricks. It could stand on its head and bark the Dog's Chorus whilst juggling eight balls on its hind paws and playing the violin with its front paws. That was just one of its tricks.

Another trick it could do was this: it would bite its own tail, then it would roll around the farmyard like a wheel, balancing two long poles on its paws – on top of one of which it was balancing Daisy the Cow and on the other Old Lob the Carthorse – all the while, at the same time, telling excruciatingly funny jokes that it made up on the spot.

One day Charlemagne, the cock, said to Stanislav the dog: 'Stan, you're wasted doing your amazing tricks here in this old farmyard – you ought to go to the Big City or join the circus.'

Stan replied: 'Maybe you're right, Charlemagne.' So one bright spring morning, Stanislav the Dog and Charlemagne the Cock set off down the road to seek their fortunes in the Big City.

They hadn't gone very far before they came to a fair. There were people selling everything you could imagine. There was also a stage on which a troupe of strolling players were performing.

So Charlemagne the Cock strode up to the leader of the troupe and said, 'Now, my good man, this is indeed your lucky day, for you see before you the most talented, most amazing juggler, acrobat, ventriloquist, comedian and all-round entertainer in the whole history of our – or any other – farmyard . . . Stanislav the Dog!' And Stanislav who all this time had been looking modestly down at his paws, now gave a low bow.

'Can't you read?' said the leader of the troupe. 'No dogs!'

And without more ado, Charlemagne the Cock and Stanislav the Dog were thrown out.

'Huh!' said Charlemagne, picking himself up and shaking the road-dust out of his feathers. 'You're too good for a troupe of strolling players anyway.'

Stanislav climbed wearily out of the ditch. He was covered in mud, and he looked at his friend very miserably.

'I'm tired,' he said. 'And I want to

go home to my master.'

'Cheer up, my friend!' replied Charlemagne the Cock. 'We're going to the Big City, where fine ladies and gentlemen drip with diamonds, where dukes and earls sport rubies and emeralds, and where the streets are paved with gold. With your talents, you'll take 'em by storm. We'll make our fortunes!'

So the cock and the dog set off once more down the long, dirty road that led to the Big City.

On the way they happened to pass a circus. Charlemagne the Cock strode up to the ringmaster, who was in the middle of teaching the lions to stand on their hind legs and jump through a ring.

'Tut! tut! tut! my good man,' said Charlemagne the Cock. 'You needn't

bother yourself with this sort of rubbish any more! Allow me to introduce you to the most superlative acrobat and tumbler – who can not only stand on his hind paws, but can jump through fifty such rings . . . backwards and whilst balancing one of your lions on his nose . . . and do it all on the high wire . . . *without a safety net*!'

'I only do tricks with lions,' said the ringmaster.

'But Stanislav the Dog has more talent in his right hind leg than your entire troupe of lions!'

'These are the best lions in the business!' exclaimed the ringmaster. 'And they'd eat you and your dog for supper without even blinking. In fact they need a feed right now!' And he reached out his hand to grab Charlemagne the Cock. Stan the Dog saw what was happening, however, and nipped the ringmaster on the ankle.

'Run, Charlemagne!' he yelled.

And Charlemagne ran as fast as he could, while Stan the Dog leapt about – nipping people's ankles – as the entire circus chased them down the road.

'Help!' squawked Charlemagne, as the circus folk got closer and closer and hands reached out to grab him by the neck.

But Stan the Dog ran under everyone's legs and tripped them up. Then he said to Charlemagne, 'Jump on my back! I can run four times as fast as these clowns!'

And so they escaped, with Charlemagne the Cock riding on Stan the Dog's back.

That night they slept under a hedge. Charlemagne the Cock was extremely nervous, but Stan the Dog curled himself around his friend to protect him. Stan himself, however, was not very happy either.

'I'm hungry,' he murmured, 'and I want to go home to my master.'

'Cheer up!' said Charlemagne. 'Tomorrow we'll reach the Great City, where your talents will be appreciated. Forget these country yokels. I'm telling you – fame and fortune await you and . . .'

But his friend was fast asleep.

Well, the next day, they arrived in the Great City. At first they were overawed by the noise and bustle. Many a time they had to leap into the gutter to avoid a cart or a carriage, and on one occasion they both got drenched when somebody emptied a chamber pot from a window above the street, and it went right over them.

'Oh dear, I miss the farmyard,' said Stan the Dog. 'And nobody here wants to know us.'

'Brace up!' cried Charlemagne. 'We're about to make our break-through! We're going straight to the top!' And he knocked on the door of the Archbishop's palace. Now it so happened that the Archbishop himself was, at that very moment, in the hallway preparing to leave the palace, and so, when the servant opened the door, the Archbishop saw the cock and the dog standing there on the step.

'Your Highness!' said Charlemagne, bowing low to the servant. 'Allow me to introduce to you the Most Amazing Prodigy Of All Time – Stanislav the Dog! He does tricks you or I would have thought impossible! They are, indeed, miracles of—'

'Clear off!' said the servant, who had been too astonished to speak for a moment. And he began to close the door.

But Charlemagne the Cock suddenly lost his temper.

'LISTEN TO ME!' he cried, and he flew at the servant with his spurs flying. Well, the servant was so surprised he fell over backwards, and Charlemagne the Cock landed on his chest and screamed, 'THIS DOG IS A GENIUS! HIS LIKE HAS NEVER BEEN SEEN OUTSIDE OUR FARMYARD! JUST GIVE HIM A CHANCE TO SHOW YOU!'

And Stan the Dog, who had nervously slunk into the hallway, started to do his trick where he bounced around on his tail, juggling precious china ornaments (which he grabbed off the sideboard as he bounced past) whilst barking a popular Farmyard Chorus that always used to go down particularly well with the pigs.

'My china!' screamed the Archbishop. 'Stop him at once!' And several of the Archbishop's servants threw themselves at Stan the Dog. But Stan bounced out of their way brilliantly, and grabbed the Archbishop's mitre and started to balance a rare old Ming vase on the top of it.

'Isn't he great?' shouted Charlemagne the Cock.

'Grab him!' screamed the Archbishop, and the servants grabbed Charlemagne.

'But look at the dog!' squawked the cock. 'Don't you see how great he is?

Do you know anyone else who can juggle like that?'

But just then – as luck would have it – all the butlers and chambermaids and kitchen skivvies and gardeners, who had heard all the noise, came bursting into the Archbishop's hall. They stood there for a moment horrified, as they watched a barking dog, bouncing around on his tail, juggling the most precious pieces of the Archbishop's prize collection of china.

'Stop him!' roared the Archbishop again. And without more ado everybody descended on poor Stan, and he disappeared under a mound of flailing arms and legs. As a result, of course, all the Archbishop's best china crashed to the floor and was smashed into smithereens.

'Now look what you've done!' yelled Charlemagne.

'Now look what *we've* done!' exclaimed the Archbishop. 'Listen to me! You're both filthy, you look as if you slept in a hedge, you stink of the chamber pot and you dare to burst into my palace and wreck my best china! Well! You're going to pay for it! Throw them into my darkest dungeons!'

And the Archbishop's servants were just about to do so, when suddenly a voice spoke from above them.

'Silence, everybody!' said the Voice.

Everybody froze. Then the Voice continued, 'Don't you know who this is? Archbishop! Shame on you! This is the Voice of God!'

The Archbishop fell to his knees, and muttered a prayer, and everyone else followed suit.

'That's better!' said the Voice of God. 'Now, let Stan the Dog go free. He didn't mean no harm.'

So they let go of Stan the Dog.

'And now,' continued the Voice of God. 'Let Charlemagne the Cock go!'

So they let go of Charlemagne the Cock.

'Now shut your eyes and wait for me to tell you to open them again!' said the Voice of God.

So they all shut their eyes, and Stan the Dog and Charlemagne the Cock fled out of the Archbishop's palace as fast as their legs could carry them.

I don't know how long the Archbishop and his servants remained kneeling there with their eyes shut, but I am certain that the Voice of God never told them to open their eyes again. For, of course, the Voice wasn't the Voice of God at all – it was the Voice of Stan the Dog.

'You are, as I say, a very talented dog,' said Charlemagne as they ran down the road. 'But I'd almost forgotten you were a ventriloquist as well!'

'Luckily for us!' replied Stan. 'But look here, Charlemagne, I'll always be talented – it's just the way I am. Only I'd rather use those talents where they're appreciated, instead of where they get us into trouble.'

'Stanislav,' said Charlemagne, 'maybe you're right.'

And so the two friends returned to the farmyard. And Stanislav the Dog continued to perform his astounding tricks for the entertainment of the other farm animals, and they always loved him.

And even though Charlemagne occasionally squawked a bit at night, and said that it was a waste of talent, Stan the Dog stayed where he was – happy to be the Star of the Farmyard.

Dick King-Smith

THINDERELLA

Once upon a time there was a tall skinny girl named Thinderella.

Her arms were like sticks and her legs were like walking sticks and an ordinary-sized dog-collar would have fitted round her middle with no trouble at all. She also had very big feet.

Thinderella had two older sisters called Gwendoline and Mirabelle, and they were as beautiful as she was plain. Handsome girls they were, with plenty of flesh on their bones, not fat but well-rounded. Buxom, you would have called them.

Gwendoline had long straight hair

as black as a raven's wing,
and Mirabelle had long
curly hair as golden as
ripe corn, and people
called them the Lovely
Sisters.

Thinderella's hair was
short and mousy, and no
one ever said
anything nice
about her.
'Scruffy thing!'
they said. 'And so
scrawny too! It's
hard to believe she's
related to the
Lovely Sisters. Why,
she goes
about in rags,

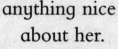

and barefoot too!'
The reason for this was
simple. Gwendoline and

Mirabelle spent lavishly upon themselves, buying all manner of expensive clothes, but they did not even allow Thinderella pocket money. Not that she had any pockets to put it in. All she got was the leftovers of food that the Lovely Sisters couldn't manage, just enough to give her the strength to do the cooking and the cleaning and the washing and the ironing and the mending.

One day a letter arrived addressed to the Misses Gwendoline and Mirabelle. It was an invitation to a Grand Ball, to celebrate the twenty-first birthday of Prince Hildebrand, the son of the King of that country.

'Look!' said Gwendoline, flourishing it under Thinderella's pinched little nose.

'But don't touch!' said Mirabelle. 'Your hands are filthy.'

'I've been doing the fires,' said
Thinderella.

'Well, go and wash,' said
Gwendoline.

'And then you can help us on with
our best clothes,' said Mirabelle. 'So
that we can go downtown.'

'And buy some even better ones for
the Ball.'

When the great night came, and the
Lovely Sisters had set off for the Ball,
sumptuously dressed and glittering
with jewellery, Thinderella sat by the
kitchen fire, staring sadly at the
glowing embers.

'How I wish I could go to the Ball,'
she whispered softly, and two big tears
ran down her grimy cheeks.

'So you shall!' said a voice.

Thinderella looked round to see a
strange little man sitting cross-legged
on the kitchen table. He had very long

hair and a big moustache and a bushy
beard, so that all Thinderella could see
of his face was a red nose and a pair
of twinkling eyes.

'Who are you?' she said.

'I,' said the little man, 'am your
Hairy Godfather, and you *shall* go to
the Ball. Run off and have a good
wash, Thinders, and put some clean
clothes on.'

'But I haven't any,' said Thinderella.

'You'll be surprised,' said the Hairy
Godfather, and sure enough when she
reached her dark attic room, there was
a ball gown laid out ready on the bed.

Quickly Thinderella washed herself, especially her feet which were very big and flat through always going about barefoot, and she put on the gown. But, she thought, I have no shoes, and then she looked under the bed and there was a pair of very large slippers, made all of glass. And she tried them on and they fitted perfectly.

Hastily Thinderella combed her short mousy hair with her newly-cleaned fingers and went downstairs again.

'Not bad,' said her Hairy Godfather. 'The gown's a bit plain, but it'll do.'

'But please,' said Thinderella, 'I'm a bit plain too. Prince Hildebrand is sure to dance the night away with Gwendoline and Mirabelle but he'll never look twice at me.'

'You'll be surprised,' said the Hairy

Godfather. 'Now then, got a pumpkin about the place?'

'No.'

'Got any mice?'

'Mice? What for?'

'Oh forget it,' said the Hairy Godfather. 'It won't take you long to walk. It's not far and it isn't raining. Have a good time. Oh, and by the way, don't stay there after midnight.'

In fact, walking even a short distance in glass slippers is murder on the feet, and by the time Thinderella arrived at the Palace, hers were agony. She hobbled into the ballroom and flopped down on a chair and stuck her thin legs out and wriggled her toes inside the glass slippers.

At that moment a young man who was walking by fell over her enormous great feet.

'Oh sorry!' gasped Thinderella.

'My fault,' said the young man. 'I wasn't looking where I was going,' and indeed Thinderella could see that he wore very thick spectacles.

'By the way,' he said, 'my name's Hildebrand,' and he stuck out a hand, vaguely in her direction.

'Oh!' she said. The Prince, she thought. He's not very handsome and he's *very* short-sighted, but he's got ever such a nice smile.

'Happy birthday,' she said.

'Oh, thanks a lot,' said the Prince.

She's got ever such a nice voice, he thought.

'I won't ask you to dance,' he said. 'I'm so clumsy, I'm always treading on people's feet.'

'You would on mine,' said Thinderella. 'They're huge,' and she took off one glass slipper and gave it to him. 'Have a look at that,' she said.

Just then Gwendoline and Mirabelle came by in all their finery, and their lovely eyes positively bulged at the sight of their sister, neatly dressed and talking to the Prince. But before they could open their lovely mouths, the clock began to strike.

'Oh gosh!' cried Thinderella. 'Midnight!' And she dashed away, leaving Prince Hildebrand holding one of the glass slippers.

In fact the clock was only striking ten, and when she got home, her Hairy Godfather was still sitting on the kitchen table, eating pickled gherkins.

'Hello, Thinders,' he said. 'You're early. What happened? Didn't the Prince look twice at you?'

'Oh, more than that,' said Thinderella. 'He's very short-sighted, you see. But he's ever so nice, Hairy

Godfather. I'm so glad I went to the Ball.'

'Good,' said the Hairy Godfather. 'And goodnight,' and he disappeared.

When Thinderella woke up next morning the ball gown and the remaining glass slipper had disappeared too, so she got up to do the housework in her usual ragged clothes. She made breakfast for the Lovely Sisters and took it up to them.

They were furious with her.

'What were you doing at the Ball?' shouted Gwendoline.

'And where did you get that gown?' yelled Mirabelle.

'And what d'you think you were doing chatting up the Prince?' they both screamed.

At that moment there was a knock at the front door.

Thinderella ran down and opened it

and there stood Prince Hildebrand, holding the other glass slipper and peering at her with his weak eyes through his thick spectacles.

'Is there anyone here whose foot will fit this slipper?' he said, coming in and tripping over the mat. 'If so, I will marry her.'

The Lovely Sisters, who had been leaning over the banisters listening, came rushing down the stairs crying 'It's mine! It's mine!' but of course when they tried it on in turn, it was far too big for their lovely little feet.

But when Thinderella put her great beetle-crusher in the slipper, it fitted perfectly!

'I told you,' she said to the Prince. 'They're huge. Don't you remember?'

How could I forget that nice voice, thought Prince Hildebrand, and he smiled his nice smile and put out his hand, vaguely in Thinderella's direction.

'I'm offering you this hand in marriage,' he said. 'Will you take it?'

And Thinderella took it, while the Lovely Sisters hurried away, their lovely faces contorted with jealous rage. So angry were they that they did not notice a little man with very long hair and a big moustache and a bushy beard, sitting cross-legged under the staircase, and grinning all over his face, or as much of it as could be seen.

The short-sighted Prince of course did not notice either, but Thinderella saw him and they winked at one another.

'By the way,' said Prince Hildebrand as his betrothed helped him down the front steps, 'I don't even know your name?'

'It's Thinderella,' said Thinderella.

'What a perfectly beautiful name,' said the Prince, blinking at her through his thick spectacles, 'for a perfectly beautiful girl.'

A CAREER IN WITCHCRAFT

'Got anythin' on a career in witchcraft?'

Mr Smike gave a heavy sigh. He was in the middle of one of his favourite tasks – noting down the names of all the people who owed library fines. He could have done without the interruption.

He set down his pen with an irritable click and peered over the desk.

'What?' he said.

'I said, got anythin' on a career in witchcraft? Please?'

The speaker was a small girl, aged

about sevenish, eightish, nineish, who cared? She stared solemnly up at him through a pair of owlish glasses. She wore a black woolly dress and a cardboard witch hat decorated with clumsily cut out moons and stars. A plastic bin liner, pinned with safety pins, hung from her shoulders. She was clutching a small broomstick.

For a brief moment, Mr Smike was taken aback. Then, he remembered. Of course. Tonight was October the thirty-first – Hallowe'en. The child was obviously all dressed up to go Trick Or Treating – an activity of which he heartily disapproved. Gangs of giggling vampires, skeletons, ghosts and masked monsters would be tramping the streets until all hours of the night, he supposed, leaning on doorbells and waving plastic bags under people's noses and demanding chocolate with menaces. Well, as far as Mr Smike was concerned, they could forget it. There would be no sweets, pennies or tangerines forthcoming from *him*. Any child unwise enough to come calling at *his* house tonight would get nothing but a stiff lecture.

'Careers over in the corner,' said Mr Smike, shortly.

'Which corner? There's four,' said the small girl.

'That one.' He jerked his head. 'And you can leave that stick here,' he ordered severely. 'I don't want bits of twig scattered all over the floor.'

For a split second, the small girl looked mutinous. Then, she gave a little nod and carefully propped her broomstick against the desk before heading off between the book racks. Mr Smike watched her, noting with disapproval that her socks had fallen down.

Mr Smike wasn't fond of children. Noisy, ill-mannered little brats with their shrill little voices and grubby little hands. The less he had to do with them, the better. Normally he would be over in the reference section of the main library, but Mrs Jaunty, the children's librarian, had rung in sick and there was nobody else to fill in.

He cast a jaundiced eye over the place. Picture books, hah! Cushions, jigsaw puzzles, mobiles, posters, murals, double hah! This wasn't a proper library. It didn't have QUIET notices all over the place. There wasn't even a box marked FINES. Great hordes of school children had been in and out all day, putting their unwashed fingers all over the books. The place had been chock-a-block with chattering mums pushing buggies full of snotty-nosed toddlers who waddled around the place getting underfoot. They treated the place like a hotel. It wasn't his kind of library at all.

Oh well. Thankfully, it was nearly closing time. With a bit of luck, that Jaunty creature would be back tomorrow, dispensing books and smiles and organising poetry competitions and story telling sessions and whatever else the silly woman did to keep the little monsters happy.

Mr Smike picked up his pen and returned to his list. Mrs C. Randall – two books, three weeks overdue at twenty pence a day, that would be eight pounds forty. Wayne Geeke, four books out on motorbike maintenance, should have been returned a month ago, that would be twenty two pounds forty and serve the cocky young lout right for having such an anti-social hobby. Old Albert Bedlam, the large print version of *Managing On A Low Income*, a full ten days overdue. Two pounds exactly. That'd make a tidy hole in his pension. J. Sugden, six books out, two weeks late, oh, excellent, excellent! Now let's see, that would be . . .

'There isn't one.'

The small girl was back again, ogling him over the desk with her magnified eyes which were, he noticed, a kind of fishy green.

'Isn't what?' snapped Mr Smike.

'A *Career in Witchcraft* book. There's nursin' and hairdressin' an' ballet dancin' an' lawyerin' an' bein' a TV presenter an' that, but nothin' on witchcraft.'

'In that case,' said Mr Smike, with great satisfaction, 'I can't help you, can I?'

There was a little pause. Mr Smike went back to his list, hoping that the annoying child would give up and go away.

'Where's the lady?' asked the small girl, standing her ground.

'At home, sick,' Mr Smike told her, with even greater satisfaction.

'The lady'd help me. She's nice. She found me lots of useful stuff. Spells and that. That's how I got my broomstick goin'. Couldn't get it to budge until she helped me find the right book. Goes like the clappers now.'

She reached out and gave the propped up broomstick a satisfied little pat.

'Indeed,' muttered Mr Smike, not looking up.

'Oh, yes. She got me a great book on *Herbs What Can Heal*. I can get rid of warts now. And boils. You got any warts or boils need fixin'?'

'No.' Mr Smike glanced pointedly at the library clock. Only another two minutes, then he could throw out this revolting child and never again have to endure her bizarre fantasies.

'Got anythin' new in on toads?' persisted his tormentor.

'No.'

'Bats?'

'No.'

'Anythin' that'll tell me where to get hold of an eye of a newt?'

'Little girl.' Mr Smike spoke wearily. He leaned forward and frowned down at her, tapping his pen. 'Little girl. Don't you think this obsession with witchcraft is a little unhealthy? What does your mother say?'

'Oh, she's all for it.' The small girl placed her elbows on the desk in what Mr Smike considered to be an over-familiar way. 'Well, she would be, wouldn't she? Bein' one herself an' that.'

'I beg your pardon?'

'Ma. She's a witch.'

'Oh, I *see*! And I suppose she's back in the cave, mixing up a brew?' enquired Mr Smike with cold sarcasm.

'Well, it's not a cave,' the small girl informed him seriously. 'This isn't the dark ages, you know. It's a proper house. But you're right about the brew. She's getting it ready for tonight's party. All me aunties are round helpin', an' cacklin' so loud I can't do me homework. Ma said to come along here an' look up stuff for meself in the library. She's trainin' me up, but she reckons you learn better if you look up stuff for yourself. An' that's what I'm doin'.'

'It's a great pity she hasn't trained you up not to tell lies, young lady,' said Mr Smike nastily. 'There are no such things as witches.' He pointed to the clock. 'See that? One minute to closing time. I suggest you remove your elbows from my desk, choose yourself a suitable book and then run along home.'

'I don't tell lies,' objected the small girl. Her green eyes flashed. 'An' there *are* such things as witches!' she added, with spirit. 'I know, 'cos I'm gonna be one. So there.'

'One minute,' repeated Mr Smike through gritted teeth.

The small girl stared at him.

'You don't believe me, do you?' she said.

'I most certainly do not believe you,' replied Mr Smike grimly. 'I've never *heard* such twaddle. Too much television, that's your trouble.'

'We haven't got a television. Ma's

got a crystal ball, but I'm not allowed to use it. Except on Saturday mornin's when she's havin' a lie in.'

Mr Smike had had enough of all this. He wagged a warning finger under the small girl's nose.

'Young lady,' he said. His voice was so sharp, you could have sliced cucumber with it. 'This is not funny. You can take a joke too far. Some people may find your flights of fancy amusing, but I am not one of them.'

There was a short silence. The small girl continued to stare at him. The clock ticked. Then:

'So you don't have anythin' on a career in witchcraft, then?'

'No!' shouted Mr Smike. 'I do not! You have no business wandering in here pestering busy adults with your ridiculous requests. You are a silly little girl with a head full of rubbish. And you can tell your mother I said so.'

The small girl went very red. There was another short silence. Then:

'I could turn you into a frog, I could,' she muttered with a scowl. And she turned abruptly on her heel and set off back down the racks.

Mr Smike felt pleased with himself. He had told her, oh yes indeed. You had to be firm with these cheeky young things. Briskly, he gathered up his papers, slipped them into his briefcase and clipped his pen into his breast pocket. He would finish the list at home. It would be something to look forward to after supper. Then, if there was time, he would write another of his complaining letters to the local paper. (Mr Smike wrote a lot of complaining letters to newspapers. It was a kind of hobby. He wrote about the state of the drains, the surliness of dustmen, the laziness of the unemployed and the trouble with Youth Today. If the paper didn't publish them, he wrote and complained about *that*.)

He opened a drawer, took out the library key in readiness and waited, eyes on the clock, tapping his foot impatiently and willing it to move on. Thirty seconds to go.

'I'll take this one,' said the small girl, appearing again and slamming a book under his nose. '*Baba Yaga*. It's got my great, great, great, great, great-gran in it. She was Russian, you know,' she added, with a certain amount of defiant pride.

'Ticket,' said Mr Smike coldly, snapping his fingers.

The small girl rummaged beneath her bin liner and slid a ticket across the desk.

Mr Smike inspected it. *Agnethia Toadfax. 13, Coldwinter Street.*

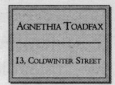

Ridiculous name for a child. But then again, the child was ridiculous, with her tacky home-made costume and overheated imagination.

To his intense disappointment, the ticket seemed to be in order. In stony silence, he stamped the book and pushed it across.

'Right,' he said curtly, pointing to the door. 'No more of your nonsense. Out.'

Agnethia Toadfax opened her mouth, seemed to be about to say something, then closed it again. She picked up her broomstick, tucked her book under her arm and marched out the door without another word.

Mr Smike shook his head and tutted for a considerable length of time.

Whatever were parents coming to these days? A good, sharp smack or two, a sight less television and a daily dose of something nasty in a spoon, that's what was needed. With a sniff, he rose, collected his coat and went to turn out the lights.

Outside, high above the library roof in the cold October night, Agnethia Toadfax hovered on her broomstick. Her hair streamed out and her bin-liner cloak flapped madly in the leaf-spinning wind. Below her, the street lamps spilled pools of orange light into the dark, empty street. Up above, wild clouds raced across the full moon.

Should she or shouldn't she? Ma had told her to be careful, to use The Power wisely and not let her temper get the better of her – but then again,

everyone was entitled to a little fun.
Especially someone who was just
setting out on a Career in Witchcraft.
And it *was* Hallowe'en . . .

'Ah, to heck with it,' she muttered,
and twiddled her fingers in a Certain
Way. Then, stifling a little giggle, she
wheeled her broomstick and headed
for home.

It went like the clappers.

Behind her and far below, Mr Smike
was struggling to turn the key in the
lock of the library door.

It was proving a difficult task.
Particularly with the thin green webs
which had suddenly sprouted between
his fingers . . .

VALENTINE

Schooldays are supposed to be the happiest days of your life, but if you're stuck with a friend like Angela Mitchell they're not. If you were an angel in Heaven she'd tempt you into mischief, and persuade you to play rude songs on your harp.

We trooped into the classroom one afternoon in February when the crocuses were out in the school garden and there was a smell of spring in the air. Miss Sopwith must have been in a good mood, because she'd decided to let us do art instead of the boring old nature lesson she'd promised us about the germination of seeds.

You know the one I mean. You have it every springtime, in every class in the school and teachers love it. You have to take a jam jar and line it with wet blotting paper and put dried peas in it so that you can watch them grow. It's supposed to be dead thrilling, seeing the little root come out, and then the little shoot, but it's pathetic if you ask me. Watching peas grow is about as exciting as watching the clothes go round in the washing machine. It's even worse than watching *Westenders* on the telly, according to my dad.

Anyway, when we sat down in our places we found that Miss Sopwith had been busy in the lunch hour putting bits of card and scissors and sticky paper out on our desks.

'I've just realized what day it is tomorrow, children,' she said, with an even soppier expression on her face than usual. 'It's a very special day. Can anybody tell me what it is?'

'Friday, Miss,' called out that great fat fool Laurence Parker, and everybody groaned.

'I mean apart from Friday, Laurence,' said Miss Sopwith. 'What else is it?'

I put my hand up but Angela beat me to it.

'It's February the 14th, Miss Sopwith,' she called out, with that beaming smile that grown-ups love so much because it makes all her dimples show. 'It's Valentine's Day.'

Miss Sopwith nodded. 'That's right, Angela,' she said. 'Saint Valentine's Day. It's a very ancient festival, which began hundreds of years ago in the fifteenth century.'

She told us about Saint Valentine,

and about how he was a martyr who was executed for his beliefs, which seems to have been the fate of most martyrs in those days, and which is probably why there aren't any left.

'He died on February the 14th,' Miss Sopwith went on. 'And so it became the custom on that day to choose a sweetheart, or a special friend, and to send them a present in memory of Saint Valentine.'

She smiled round at the class.

'Of course we send cards rather than presents these days,' she said. 'And I know you're much too young for sweethearts . . .'

She held up her hand for silence as the boys started to stamp their feet and snigger and boo, while some of the girls giggled and nudged one another.

'But I'm sure you all have a special

friend you'd like to send a card to,'
Miss Sopwith continued when the
noise died down. 'So I thought it
would be nice if we made some this
afternoon. And to make it more of a
challenge, I want you to write a
message inside your card which
matches the design on the front.'

You could tell that the boys thought
it was Old Soppy's soppiest idea yet,
but as they had no choice in the
matter they settled down after a
minute and we all got on with it. And
I found I quite enjoyed the work once
I'd started.

I used a design that I'd seen in the
paper shop only a few days before.
First of all I cut out a big red heart
from sticky paper and stuck that in the
middle of the card. Then I cut a long
strip from a lace paper doily and stuck
that down all round the edge of the

heart like a lacy frill. It took me ages
to draw tiny roses in all the spaces I
had left, and to colour them in with
red and pink and yellow felt pens, but
it was worth it, because the card
looked really lovely.

When it was finished I sharpened
my pencil and in my very best writing
I wrote a message inside that I
thought was rather neat because of
the heart on the front.

Happy Valentines Day

From the bottom of my heart

'That's beautiful, Charlotte,' said Miss Sopwith. 'I'm sure your special friend will be delighted to receive that.'

Everybody leaned over and craned their necks to look, and there was a chorus of oohs and ahs. I glanced round at Angela who sits in the row behind me. She grinned at me and winked, confident that I had only one special friend and that it was her.

I grinned back, but I didn't really mean it. I still hadn't forgiven her for putting that horrible black slug in my desk the day before. If she thought I was going to send a Valentine to her she had another think coming. I'd send it to that nice David Watkins instead. It would serve her right.

I made an envelope from the sheet of white paper Miss Sopwith had provided, and sealed the card up in it.

I would ask my mum for a stamp when I got home, I decided, writing David's name and address on the front. Then I slipped it into my desk so that nobody would see.

The lesson was almost over and it was getting noisy again, with everybody showing their cards to one another and laughing and jeering. Cleverclogs Laurence Parker had drawn a picture of an enormous whale, with '*We could have a WHALE of a time together!*' written inside. David Watkins had drawn a sweet little furry bear, and the message inside was '*I couldn't BEAR to be without you!*' All the girls were cooing over it, and you could tell they each hoped he'd send it to them.

Angela's card was a mess. She's not very good at drawing or cutting out, and she had only managed to make a sort of house with a door in the middle and a window at each side of the door, like they do in the babies' class. Inside she'd written '*Come to my HOUSE for tea one day!*', which Miss Sopwith didn't think was very clever at all.

'Oh dear, Angela. Couldn't you make a better effort than that?' she tutted, and Angela scowled and shoved the card in the rubbish bin, because she hates anyone to be better than her.

The bell rang for afternoon play-time and we all clattered to our feet, but Old Soppy made us sit down again because she had something important to say.

'I just want to remind you that Miss Collingwood will be showing visitors round the school tomorrow, and she wants you all to look clean and smart.' She peered at us severely over her spectacles. 'No scruffy jeans or trainers, please, boys,' she said. 'And no fancy socks or leg-warmers, girls, if you don't mind.'

One or two of the girls went pink and hid their feet under their desks because there had been a craze recently for wearing all sorts of stripy, coloured and patterned socks and leg-warmers to school. My mum wouldn't let me wear anything but grey, but Angela had been turning up in all sorts of things, including socks with Mickey Mouse on, and bright pink fluffy leg-warmers that made her look like a flamingo.

Miss Sopwith got up from her desk. 'I know school uniform isn't strictly compulsory in the junior classes,' she said. 'But it would look nice if you could all wear it on this occasion. And that means you, too, Angela, if you don't mind.'

She dismissed the class and we all charged out into the playground like a herd of animals escaping from the zoo. Angela followed more slowly, a brooding expression on her face.

'She's a stupid old bat,' she glowered, joining me by the gate. 'There was no need to pick on me. Plenty of other people wear fancy socks.'

She glared at the classroom window, where Miss Sopwith could be seen putting out a row of jam jars on the sill. It looked as if we were going to get that nature lesson after all.

'And she needn't have been so rude about my Valentine card, either,' said Angela. 'Stupid old bat.'

'Well, it wasn't very good, was it?' I said reasonably. 'A five-year-old could do better.'

I could have bitten my tongue out as soon as I said it, for Angela directed that icy blue gaze on me and gave me a look that turned my insides to frozen chicken livers. Then she went stomping off.

I watched nervously as she gathered all the other girls in our class into a huddle in a corner of the playground. I knew she was plotting some kind of revenge, because that awful Delilah Jones kept looking at me over her shoulder and giggling, while Angela whispered into her ear.

I worried all the rest of the afternoon, and I didn't listen to one word of the nature lesson, even though Miss Sopwith had been really inventive this time and had provided beans instead of peas for a change. Only half of my mind was in the classroom, while the other half was trying to guess what Angela was cooking up. It was bound to be something nasty, I felt sure.

The bell rang for home-time at last. After a final reminder from Miss Sopwith about school uniform, we were let out. I collected my Valentine card from my desk and set off home by myself, but to my astonishment Angela ran after me and pushed her arm through mine, as nice as ninepence.

'You can give me that Valentine now, if you like,' she said. 'It'll save you posting it.'

I shook my arm free. 'It's not for you,' I told her. 'I know you've been plotting to get me into trouble. So you can just get lost, Angela Mitchell. I'm going to send it to David Watkins, if my mum'll give me a stamp.'

Angela looked hurt. 'We weren't plotting anything against you, Charlie, honest,' she said. 'We were planning our revenge on Soppy Sopwith for being such a stupid old bat.'

I scowled at her suspiciously. 'So why did you keep me out of it?' I demanded. 'Why did you tell all the others, and not me?'

She looked even more hurt. 'You're always saying you don't want to be involved in any mischief. I thought you wouldn't want anything to do with it. And anyway, I'm telling you now, aren't I?'

So I walked home with her while she told me the plan, and it was the craziest thing I'd ever heard. In spite of what Miss Sopwith had said about school uniform, all the girls had agreed to wear coloured socks and leg-warmers to school the next day.

'That'll show her she can't boss us around,' crowed Angela gleefully, as we turned the corner into our road. 'And it won't half show her up in front of Miss Collingwood and her visitors.'

'You can't do that,' I said. 'Not after Miss Sopwith asked us specially. She'll be furious.'

'Of course she will,' said Angela. 'That's the whole point. And there won't be a thing she can do about it, will there? She said herself that uniform isn't compuncshunry in the junior school.'

I couldn't help giggling at that.

'There's no such word as compuncshunry,' I told her. 'You mean compulsory.'

'That's what I said,' she assured me, quite unabashed. 'Compulshunry. So be sure to wear your lovely purple and green stripy socks tomorrow, won't you?'

We stopped at the front gate of Angela's house, which is next door to mine, and she snatched the Valentine card from my hand.

'I'll post that for you, Charlie,' she said. 'I've got a first class stamp. And I'm going to Barlow with my mum, so I can make sure it doesn't miss the last post.' And off she went into the house.

I wasn't very happy about it, but it was too late to stop her. She'll probably forget to post it, I told myself gloomily, as I let myself in the back door. Just to get her own back. And all that work will have been for nothing.

But I wasn't fooled by her so-called revenge on Miss Sopwith. When I thought it over it stuck out a mile that it was only another of her tricks to get me into trouble. I was supposed to turn up in stripy socks, and I was meant to be the only one. Well, this time I wasn't going to fall for it. I'd wear my grey school socks the next day, and be a step ahead of her for once.

The next morning I dressed in my uniform as usual and went downstairs. My dad was making breakfast and my mum was reading the paper at the kitchen table. I helped myself to some Sugar Crunchies, then I jumped up from the table again as the letterbox rattled in the hall.

There were three Valentine cards. One for each of us. One for my dad from my mum. One for my mum from my dad. And one for me without a signature. A card with a sweet cuddly bear on it, and the words, '*I couldn't BEAR to be without you!*' written inside.

My mum and dad started the usual

soppy kissing and cooing stuff, so I quickly swallowed the rest of my breakfast and set off for school. I was so happy I almost floated round the corner into Angela's drive. I couldn't wait to see her face when I told her that out of all the girls in the class David Watkins had sent his Valentine card to me.

I forgot all about Valentines the minute I saw her. She was coming out of the house to meet me, her satchel over her shoulder, wearing her grey school coat and black shoes, and her FLUFFY FLAMINGO-COLOURED LEG-WARMERS.

'Oh, Charlie!' she laughed, looking at my feet. 'You are a wimp. You'll be the only one in grey socks, and everybody will laugh at you.'

She was right. As we walked to school we met more and more girls from our class going in the same direction. The new girl, Jane McLachlan, who moved here last year from Scotland and talks in a lovely Scottish voice. The twins, Jenny and Josie Brown, who look so much alike that even their mother gets them mixed up. That awful spiteful Delilah Jones, who pinches you and laughs when you squeal. And my heart sank

deeper and deeper into my stomach because not one of them was wearing grey school socks. They were all wearing coloured tights, stockings or leg-warmers, of all colours of the rainbow.

Everybody scoffed and jeered when they saw me. They called me a namby-pamby and a goody-goody and a teacher's pet. My face burned and I felt like crawling under a stone.

We had almost reached the school gates when Angela took pity on me.

'Here, Charlie,' she said, rummaging in her satchel. 'I guessed you might chicken out, so I've brought you some of mine.' And she held out a big red bundle that turned out to be a pair of enormous woolly socks of the brightest shade of scarlet you ever saw.

I knew Miss Sopwith wouldn't be pleased, but anything was better than being an outcast in the classroom, so I sat down on a low wall and let Angela help me change. The socks were so thick I could hardly get my shoes back on, and they were so long and heavy that when I stood up they drooped in folds around my ankles, but the other girls cheered when they saw me putting them on and I felt like one of the gang again.

The school bell rang and Angela grabbed my grey socks and stuffed them into her satchel.

'Come on, Charlie,' she urged. 'We don't want to be late.'

She ran off with the others and I followed them into school, wondering why Angela and Delilah Jones were giggling so much. It was only when I was putting my coat on its peg in the cloakroom that I realized what an idiot I had been. After hanging up their coats all the girls from my class sat down on the benches round the walls and peeled off their coloured tights and leg-warmers, revealing grey school uniform socks underneath.

Angela danced about laughing when she saw my face.

'What a proper Charlie you are, Charlie!' she giggled. 'You fall for it every time!' The other girls gathered round and giggled too, while I stood there in those stupid great red socks feeling like the biggest fool in the whole universe.

Then the second bell rang, and the cloakroom began to empty as most of the girls ran off to the classroom. Jenny Brown came and put her arm round my shoulders, frowning at Angela.

'You are going to give Charlie her socks back now, Angela?' she said severely. 'You promised you would. Otherwise none of us would have agreed to the trick.'

Angela looked indignant. 'Of course I am,' she said, delving into her satchel. 'What do you take me for? It was only a joke.'

Jenny smiled at me and went after the others. I pulled off the red socks and hopped impatiently from one bare foot to the other while Angela rummaged about in her satchel, muttering and shaking her head, and spilling things out onto the floor.

'They're not here, Charlie,' she said at last. 'They must have fallen out somewhere on the way into school.'

I stared at her, aghast.

'What am I going to do?' I squeaked. 'I can't go in with no socks on. Miss Sopwith will kill me!'

Angela smiled that special smile,

sweet with something nasty lurking in it, like the medicine Dr Locke gave me when I had the 'flu.

'Sorry, but you'll have to, Charlie,' she said airily. 'It's the red ones or none at all. It's up to you.' And she walked off.

In the end I chose to wear none at all, and I had a hard time explaining to Miss Sopwith, I can tell you. All I could say was that I'd lost them, and I couldn't blame her for not believing me. She gave me a right telling-off, and made me sit with my feet in a cardboard box until Miss Collingwood and her visitors had been round the school.

The other kids felt dead sorry for me, and some of them helped me to look for my socks at playtime. David Watkins found them at last, stuffed behind the bench near the gate, but when I tried to thank him he went all red and embarrassed and wouldn't even look at me. It was something to do with my Valentine card, I felt sure, because I had seen him showing it to the other boys in the corner by the wall. They all burst out laughing when they saw it, and I felt awful when I saw him crumple it up and throw it away in the bin.

I found out why when Laurence Parker nudged my arm on the way back into school.

'That was a brill card you sent to David Watkins,' he chuckled admiringly. 'I didn't know you could be so rude.'

'Rude?' I said, astonished. 'What was rude about it?'

He wouldn't tell me, so I hung back as everybody went inside. I went to the dustbin and retrieved the card, shaking off the toffee papers and crisp crumbs and smoothing out the wrinkles with my hand.

I almost stopped breathing when I read it, for my message had been rubbed out and replaced with another. In Angela's unmistakable careless scrawl, the card now said,

Happy Valintines Day

From the hart of

my bottom

Roger Collinson

WILLY
AND THE UFO

Willy saw a lot of Grandad. He ran
errands for him; he took messages
from his mum; and each week he
collected Grandad's science-fiction
magazines and papers from the
newsagent. There were a lot of them,
and Grandad read them from cover to
cover.

'Today's science-fiction is
tomorrow's science-fact,' he told Willy.
'When I was a kid, landing on the
moon was just a story. And now it's
history. And the things you see today
in Star Trek – they'll happen, Willy. I

may not live to see it, but you will.'

Willy was not as sure as Grandad abut all that; but it cost him nothing to say, 'Gosh! Wow! Really, Grandad?'

The thing which particularly interested Grandad, the thing which really got him going, was UFOs. Just in case you don't know what that means, I'll tell you. The letters stand for 'Unidentified Flying Object'. All over the world, it seems, people are seeing things whizzing about the sky which can't be aeroplanes, or weather balloons, or anything we know. And a lot of people say that these Unidentified Flying Objects are spacecraft from other planets.

Grandad was convinced of this. He could tell Willy dozens of stories of people who had actually seen UFOs land, talked to the crews, and even been taken for rides. If Grandad could be granted just one wish, Willy knew that it would be to see a UFO. And Willy wished that he could make Grandad's wish come true.

Often Grandad went out looking for a UFO.

'People who are looking,' Grandad said, 'are more likely to see than people who are not . . . stands to reason!'

And so, armed with binoculars and a notebook, he would puff to the top of one of the hills outside town and spend hours staring up at the sky, hoping to spot a UFO. Sometimes he would go by day, and sometimes he would do his spotting by night, when, in addition to the binoculars and notebook, he took a torch.

Willy had kept him company on a couple of these trips – during the day, of course – but, to tell the truth, he found them pretty boring. If, after five minutes of gazing up at the sky, you haven't seen a UFO, you begin to think of more interesting ways to pass the next five minutes.

Now, it happened that Grandad's birthday fell on a Sunday, and, after dinner, Willy went round to him with a fruit cake from his mum and a pair of pointy, rubber, Vulcan ears you could put on over your own ears. He'd got them second-hand for 10p at a school jumble sale. Willy arrived at Grandad's just as Grandad was opening the front door to leave. Willy saw the binoculars and notebook and he knew that Grandad was going to celebrate his Seventy-Fifth with a bit of UFO-spotting. The presentation of the cake delayed things for a bit, and the trying-on of the ears, which made Grandad look more like a garden gnome than Mr Spock.

'Well,' said Grandad, when the cake had been put into a tin and the ears propped up on the mantelpiece, 'I'm going to the tops for a bit. Coming?'

The sun was shining, and it was Grandad's birthday, so Willy said he'd go. They made an odd pair: Grandad in his Starship uniform and Willy in his shorts, big enough for two boys, or even three – but *that* would have been a squeeze. They left the streets and houses behind them, and laboured up a hill. Larks twittered high above them, just tiny dots in a sky empty of all cloud. If any UFO was out for an afternoon spin round the universe and passed that way, it would be spotted easily.

At the top of the hill, Grandad sat down. In his notebook he recorded the date and time, and then he began to search the sky through his binoculars. Willy lay down beside him and gazed up into the blue. But, apart from the larks, there was nothing doing. The warm sunshine and the stillness were very relaxing, and it wasn't long before Grandad said, 'I'm just going to rest my eyes for a couple of minutes. You can have the binoculars, Willy, and keep watch.' Then he lay down, and, within moments, the handkerchief which he had spread over his face was rising and falling to his snores.

Willy enjoyed playing with the binoculars. He didn't waste much time looking up into the sky because there was nothing there. But it was fun looking back into the town where you could see people walking, gardening, cleaning the car – but all silently, like TV with the sound turned down. And Willy was so occupied in watching the progress of a dog as it followed its nose from lamppost to pillar box to telegraph pole that he did not see the UFO until it was within a metre of touching down.

Have you ever watched a soap bubble floating through the air? The UFO was something like that. But about as big as a bus. You couldn't actually see through it, but it so reflected air and sky that it seemed almost not to be there at all. Noiselessly, it landed only half-a-dozen steps from Willy. The binoculars had fallen into his lap, and he stared with his mouth hanging open like – as his school teacher once put it – like a litter bin.

The UFO sat there on the turf and nothing happened. Willy gulped and tried to say, 'Grandad!' But not a syllable could he pronounce. And

Grandad snored on.

At this point, you might expect a panel to slide open or steps to be lowered for aliens to walk down. Aliens, when they did emerge, did not use doors or steps; they seemed to melt through the bubble the way ghosts are supposed to be able to glide through walls. Three aliens came out of the UFO and stood in front of Willy. You will want to know what they were like. You will be hoping for something really extraordinary; but I have to disappoint you. The aliens were little and they were green.

All three were looking hard at Willy, and he could hear them talking about him. It was rather like listening to a Walkman: their voices sounded inside his head.

'*Blimey!*' said one of them. This was the word Willy heard, because he was

tuned into the aliens' thought waves
and he heard them in English – *his*
English. Mr Wheaton, his teacher, or
Reverend Entwhistle, the vicar, would
have heard something more refined.

'Flaming Norah!' exclaimed the
second.

'It's an ugly specimen, ain't it?' said
the third.

'Well, I wouldn't like to meet it on a
dark night by myself – and that's for
sure!'

'And that great gob! It's like
something to throw rubbish in!'

'Certainly a very primitive life
form. The brain cavity must be
minute.'

Willy, who was beginning to
recover from the shock, was stung by
these remarks. It was one thing for
smarty school teachers to be sarcastic
at his expense, but he was blowed if he

was going to take it sitting down from a bunch of little green men. So he stood up.

'Hel–lo!' said one of the aliens. 'Here comes trouble!'

'Immobiliser, Chief?' said another.

'Yeah – Force 2 should do the trick; and then we'll transport it aboard.'

Willy started to say, 'Oi! Just you watch it, mate!' when the second alien took something like a ballpoint pen from his tunic and pointed it at him. A long, lazy tickle started at his toes and rose up through his body to the roots of his hair. It left him frozen like a game of Statues, with a raised fist and, on his face, a soppy grin. And the next thing he knew he was drifting above the grass and melting through the side of the UFO.

From the outside, the UFO had looked pretty big. Inside it was immense. Although Willy could not turn his head to look about him, he could see various levels and dozens of little green men bustling hither and thither, travelling up and down on escalators, operating banks of instruments, and putting their heads together in urgent discussion.

A little green man, distinguished by a red, shiny belt, approached the three who had brought Willy into the UFO.

'Ah, you've got one!' he said. 'Hmmm!' He walked round Willy. 'Not very promising, I'd say. Still, I suppose we'd better have it analysed. If we don't go by the book, there'll be hell to pay. You know what they're like back at Control.' Willy's captors sighed and nodded. 'Yes,' Red Belt went on, 'regulations is regulations. "*At each planet visited, a specimen of the dominant life-force shall be taken and*

assessed for its potential usefulness . . ."
Well, I could tell them here and now
that it'll take another thousand light
years of evolution before *this* would be
worth putting in a tin of cat's food!'

The other three 'Ho – ho – ho'd' at
their boss's little joke.

'OK, take it up to the lab. Oh, and
tell them to be more careful this time.
We're supposed to put them back just
the way they were when we picked
them up.'

Willy did not like the sound of this.
He was still hovering a couple of
centimetres from the floor, and now
the aliens pushed him effortlessly into
a transportation tube. In this he was
whooshed up several floors, and found
himself in a small room where only
half a dozen aliens were working. Two
of these manoeuvred him onto a kind
of circular platform.

'Right-ho, flower!' called an alien with silver cuffs to his tunic. 'You can free the poor lamb now.'

An amber light played on Willy from above, and he felt his muscles relaxing.

'Just stay where you are, poppet,' Silver Cuffs said to him. 'This won't take very long, and you won't feel anything – hardly.'

Then he walked round Willy as Red Belt had done. 'Well, well, well!' he sighed. 'Only a mother could love it! But don't you just *adore* the trousers! They're so deliciously awful! My friend, Derf, at the museum would love them for his collection of inter-galactic costumes.'

'Well, he ain't having them!' Willy declared, indignantly.

'Oh, it's all right, sweetie,' said Silver Cuffs. 'We make duplicates of

anything we want to take back . . .
OK!' he called to his assistants. 'Ready
when you are.'

A transparent cylinder came down
from the ceiling, and Willy found
himself trapped inside it like a goldfish
in a pickle jar.

There was a humming which rose to a whistle; light flickered through every colour of the rainbow; and Willy felt a tingling and a weightlessness as though the atoms of his body had been separated – as indeed they had – and were floating freely inside the cylinder. Then the whistle fell back to a hum, and the light steadied to a constant beam again. The transparent cylinder was raised, and Willy stood there, blinking and swallowing hard.

'There now,' said Silver Cuffs. 'That didn't hurt, did it? . . . and I *think* everything's back in its proper place.'

The first thing Willy checked was his trousers. To his immense relief, they were still there, sagging from the braces as they always were. Then he anxiously examined his hands, and checked ears and nose with his fingers. Other things would have to wait. But, as far as he could tell, all was as it should be.

'Now, usually,' said Silver Cuffs, 'we'd take you on a flight – give you a bit of a thrill and all that. But, it seems, the old one is about to come to, so we'll just have to pop you back straightaway . . . 'Byee!'

And, in a trice, Willy was sitting beside Grandad again, and staring, goggle-eyed, at the UFO, which rose swiftly from the earth and, in moments, was lost to view.

Grandad puffed and snorted and pulled the hanky from his face. He sat up, still heavy with sleep, and, when he remembered where he was, he turned to Willy, who was gawping at the empty sky.

'Why aren't you using the binoculars, Willy?' Grandad said, irritably. 'Increases your chances of seeing something.'

'I have!' Willy croaked, with his eyes still fixed on empty space.

'Have *what*?' said Grandad.

'Seen something . . . I've seen a UFO!'

'Now, stop messing me about,' said Grandad. 'This is serious scientific research we're doing.'

'But, Grandad . . . !' said Willy. And he tried to describe all that had happened to him. Grandad only got crosser and crosser.

'Bubbles and little green men! Never heard anything so daft in all my life!' But he peered hopefully at the sky. 'Oh, come on!' he said. 'I need a cup of tea and a slice of that cake your mother sent.'

Willy woke in the middle of the night – unusual for him – but the room was not in total darkness. From the corner where Willy dropped his clothes when he undressed came a greenish glow. And, when Willy got out of bed to take a closer look, he found it was not coming from his shoes, or socks, or pants, or T-shirt, but only from his trousers.

'*We make duplicates of anything we want to take,*' Silver Cuffs had said. And Willy had assumed it was the duplicates they took back with them. But, as he held his trousers by the braces and their green light played gently on his face, he knew that he was wrong.

At the same time, a group of little green men were standing in front of a cabinet in which Willy's trousers were displayed. Beside them was a picture of Willy himself, wearing the trousers; and a notice gave details of where the exhibit had been collected.

The little green men gazed at Willy's trousers with their tiny mouths wide with astonishment. And then their laughter echoed round the galleries of the museum, until an attendant told them to be quiet.

V. H. Drummond

THE
FLYING POSTMAN

Mr Musgrove was a Postman in a
village called Pagnum Moss.

Mr and Mrs Musgrove lived in a
house called Fuchsia Cottage. It was
called Fuchsia Cottage because it had
a fuchsia hedge round it. In the front
garden they kept a cow called Nina,
and in the back garden they grew
strawberries . . . nothing else but
strawberries.

Now Mr Musgrove was no ordinary
Postman; for instead of walking or
trundling about on a bicycle, he flew
around in a Helicopter. And instead of

pushing letters in through letter boxes, he tossed them into people's windows, singing as he did so, 'Wake up! Wake up! For morning is here!'

Thus people were able to read their letters quietly in bed without littering them untidily over the breakfast table.

Sometimes to amuse the children, Mr Musgrove tied a radio set to the tail of the Helicopter, and flew about in time to the music. He had a special kind of Helicopter that was able to loop the loop and even fly UPSIDE DOWN!

But one day the Postmaster-General and the Postal Authorities sent for Mr Musgrove and said, 'It is forbidden to do stunts in the sky. You must keep the Helicopter only for delivering letters and parcels, and not for playing about!'

Mr Musgrove felt crestfallen.

After that Mr Musgrove put his Helicopter away when he had finished work, till one day some of the children came to him and said, 'Please do a stunt in the sky for us, Mr Musgrove!'

When he told them he would never do any more stunts, the children felt very sad and some even cried a little. Mr Musgrove could not bear to see little children sad, so he tied the radio set to the Helicopter, and jumping into the driving seat flew swiftly into the air, to a burst of loud music.

'I'll do just one trick,' he said to himself, 'a new, and very special one!'

The children stopped crying and jumped gaily up and down.

He flew high, high, high up into the sky till he was almost out of sight, then he came whizzing down and swooped low, low, low over the church steeple and away again.

The children, who had scrambled onto a nearby roof top to get a better view, cried, 'It's a lovely trick! Do it again! PLEASE do it again!'

So Mr Musgrove flew high, high, high into the sky again and came whizzing and swooping down low, low, low . . . But this time he came TOO low and . . . landed with a whizz! Wang! DONC! right on the church steeple.

The Postmaster-General, from his house on the hill, heard the crash and came galloping to the spot on his horse, Black Bertie. The Postal Authorities also heard the crash, and came running to the spot, on foot.

When he got to the church the Postmaster-General dismounted from Black Bertie and, waving his fist at Mr Musgrove, said sternly, 'This is a very serious offence! Come down at once!'

'I can't,' said Mr Musgrove, unhappily, '. . . I'm stuck!'

So the Postal Authorities got a strong ladder and climbed up the steeple and lifted Mr Musgrove and the Helicopter down.

When they got to the ground, they examined Mr Musgrove's arms and legs and saw that nothing was broken. They also noticed that the radio set was intact. But the poor Helicopter was seriously damaged; its tail was drooping, its nose was pushed up, and its whole system was badly upset.

'It will take weeks to mend!' said the Postal Authorities.

The Postmaster–General turned to Mr Musgrove and said: 'For this you will be dismissed from the Postal Service. Hand me your uniform.'

Mr Musgrove sadly handed him his peaked hat and his little jacket that had red cord round the edges.

'Mr Boodle will take your place,' said the Postmaster-General.

Mr Boodle was the Postman from the next village. He did not like the idea of delivering letters for two villages. 'Too much for one man on a bicycle,' he grumbled, but not loud enough for the Postmaster-General to hear.

Mr Musgrove went back to Fuchsia Cottage in his waistcoat.

'I've lost my job, Mrs Musgrove,' he said.

Even Nina looked sad and her ears flopped forward.

'Never mind,' said Mrs Musgrove, 'we will think of a new job for you.'

'I am not very good at doing anything except flying a Helicopter and delivering letters,' said Mr Musgrove.

So they sat down to think and think, and Nina thought too, with her own special cow-like thoughts.

After a while Mrs Musgrove had a Plan.

'We will pick the strawberries from the back garden and with the cream from Nina's milk we will make some Pink Ice Cream and sell it to people passing by,' she cried.

'What a wonderful plan!' shouted Mr Musgrove, dancing happily round. 'You *are* clever, Mrs Musgrove!'

Nina looked as if she thought it was a good idea, too, and said 'Moo-oo!'

The next day Mr Musgrove went gaily into the back garden and picked a basketful of strawberries. He was careful not to eat any himself, but put them *all* into the basket. Mrs Musgrove milked Nina and skimmed off the cream. And together they made some

lovely Pink Ice Cream. Then they put
up a notice:

```
PINK ICE CREAM
FOR SALE
```

Nina looked very proud.

When the children saw the notice
they ran eagerly in to buy. And even a
few grown-ups came, and said, 'Num,
Num! What elegant Ice Cream!'

By evening they had sold out, so
they turned the board round. Now
it said:

```
PINK ICE CREAM
TOMORROW
```

Every day they made more Pink Ice Cream and every evening they had sold out.

'We are beginning to make quite a lot of lovely money,' said Mr Musgrove.

But though they were so successful with their Pink Ice Cream, Mr Musgrove often thought wistfully of the Helicopter, and his Postman's life. One day as he was exercising Nina in the woods near his home, he met Mr Boodle. Mr Boodle grumbled that he had too much work to do.

'I would rather be a bicycling postman than no postman at all,' sighed Mr Musgrove.

Early one morning before the Musgroves had opened their Ice Cream Stall, Nina saw the Postmaster-General riding along the road on his horse, Black Bertie. Nina liked Black

Bertie, so as they passed she thrust her head through the fuchsia hedge and said, 'Moo ooo.'

Black Bertie was so surprised that he shied and reared up in the air . . . and tossed the Postmaster-General into the fuchsia hedge.

'Moo,' said Nina, in alarm, and Mr and Mrs Musgrove came running up.

Carefully they carried him into the house. They laid him on a sofa and put smelling salts under his nose, and tried to make him take some strong, sweet tea, and a little brandy.

But nothing would revive him.

They tried practically everything, including chocolate biscuits and fizzy lemonade, but he never stirred, till Mrs Musgrove came towards him carrying a Pink Ice Cream.

'What's that?' he said, opening one eye, 'it smells good.'

So they gave him one.

'It's delicious!' he cried. 'Delicious!'

They gave him another and another and another . . .

He ate SIX!

'I have recovered now,' he said, standing up, 'thanks to your elegant ice creams, which are the best I have ever tasted!'

Then he walked outside and called Black Bertie, who had walked into the garden and was eating the grass with Nina. 'Come on, Black Bertie, we must go home,' he said, and jumped into the saddle and rode away, waving his hand graciously to the Musgroves.

That afternoon, much to the Musgroves' surprise, he reappeared again. Nina was careful not to moo through the fuchsia hedge at Black Bertie this time.

'I have reappeared,' said the

Postmaster-General, 'because I am so grateful for your kindness and your ice creams that I have prepared a little surprise for you up at my house. Would you like to come and see it, Mr Musgrove?'

'Why, yes!' cried Mr Musgrove, wondering excitedly what on earth it could be.

'Jump on, then!' cried the Postmaster-General. 'I am afraid there isn't room for Mrs Musgrove too.'

At first Mr Musgrove felt a bit nervous of Black Bertie, but he was too excited to see what the Postmaster-General's surprise was really to care.

When they arrived at the Postmaster-General's house they put Black Bertie away and gave him a piece of sugar. Then the Postmaster-General led Mr Musgrove up the steps of the house into the hall, where stood a large wooden chest. He opened the chest, and drew out . . . Mr Musgrove's peaked cap and little blue jacket with red cord round the edges!

He handed the uniform to Mr Musgrove. 'Please wear this,' he said, 'and become once more the Flying Postman of Pagnum Moss!'

Mr Musgrove was very excited and thanked the Postmaster-General three times. Then the Postmaster-General took him out into the garden. 'Look!' he said, pointing at the lawn, and there stood the Helicopter all beautifully mended!

'Jump in!' cried the Postmaster-General. 'And be on duty tomorrow morning.'

Mr Musgrove raced across the lawn and leaped gleefully in. As he was flying away the Postmaster-General called, 'Will you sell me six of your beautiful Pink Ice Creams every day, and deliver them to me with the letters every morning?'

'Most certainly!' cried Mr Musgrove, leaning out of the Helicopter and saluting.

'Six Pink Ice Creams . . . I'll keep them in my refrigerator. Two for my lunch, two for my tea and two for my dinner!' shouted the Postmaster-General.

Imagine Mrs Musgrove's and Nina's surprise when Mr Musgrove alighted in the front garden, fully dressed in Postman's clothes.

'I'm a Postman again!' he cried. 'Oh, happy day!'

'Moo-oo,' cried Nina, and Mrs Musgrove clapped her hands.

The next morning he set out to deliver letters and to sing his song,

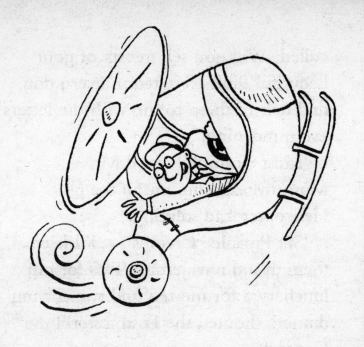

'Wake up! Wake up! For morning is here!' and everyone woke up and shouted, 'Mr Musgrove, the Flying Postman, is back in the sky again! Hurrah, Hooray!'

Mr Boodle, the grumbling postman, said, 'Hurrah, Hooray!' too, because now he would not have so much work to do. He was so excited that he took his hands off the handlebars, and then he took his feet off the pedals till the Postmaster-General passed by and, pointing at him said, 'That is dangerous and silly.'

So he put his hands back on the handlebars and his feet back on the pedals.

Mr Musgrove never forgot to bring the Postmaster-General the six Pink Ice Creams; two for his lunch, two for his tea and two for his dinner. And every day clever Mrs Musgrove made

Pink Ice Cream all by herself, till soon
they had enough money to buy a little
Helicopter of their very own, which
they called FLITTERMOUSE. They had
Flittermouse made with a hollow in
the back for Nina to sit in, and on
Saturdays they went to the city to
shop, and on Sundays they went for a
spin.

Often Mr Musgrove did musical sky
stunts in Flittermouse for the children,
but he was careful never to fly low
over the church steeple.

ACKNOWLEDGEMENTS

Random House Children's Books are grateful for permission to reproduce the following copyright stories in this anthology:

Robert Swindells, 'You Can't Bring That in Here' from *Snake on a Bus*, edited by Val Bierman (Methuen Children's Books, 1994), © Robert Swindells, 1994. Reproduced by permission of the Jennifer Luithlen Agency on behalf of the author.

Allan Ahlberg, 'Too Many Bears' from *Ten in a Bed* by Allan Ahlberg & André Amstutz (Granada Publishing, 1983), text © Allan Ahlberg, 1983. Reproduced by permission of Penguin Books Ltd.

Mick Gowar, 'The Amazing Talking Pig' from *The Amazing Talking Pig and Other Stories* (Hamish Hamilton, 1993), © Mick Gowar, 1993. Reproduced by permission of David Higham Associates Ltd on behalf of the author.

Emily Rodda, *Bob and the House Elves* (Bloomsbury Publishing Plc, 2001), © Emily Rodda, 1998. Reproduced by permission of Bloomsbury Publishing Plc.

Terry Jones, 'The Star of the Farmyard' from *Fantastic Stories* by Terry Jones with illustrations by Michael Foreman (Pavilion Books Ltd, 1992), text © Terry Jones, 1992. Reproduced by permission of Chrysalis Children's Books.

Dick King-Smith, 'Thinderella' from *The Topsy-Turvy Storybook* by Dick King-Smith with illustrations by John Eastwood (Victor Gollancz, 1992), text © Fox Busters Ltd, 1992. Reproduced by permission of Penguin Books Ltd.

Kaye Umansky, 'A Career in Witchcraft' from *Stacks of Stories*, edited by Mary Hoffman (Hodder Children's Books in collaboration with the Library Association, 1997), © Kaye Umansky, 1997. Reproduced by permission of the Caroline Sheldon Literary Agency Ltd on behalf of the author.

Sheila Lavelle, 'Valentine' (Chapter 1) from *Calamity with the Fiend* (Hamish Hamilton, 1993), © Sheila Lavelle, 1993. Reproduced by permission of Penguin Books Ltd.

Roger Collinson, 'Willy and the UFO' from *Willy and the UFO and Other Stories* (Andersen Press Limited, 1995), © Roger Collinson, 1995. Reproduced by permission of Andersen Press Ltd.

V. H. Drummond, 'The Flying Postman' from *A Golden Land* edited by James Reeves (Puffin Books, 1973), © V. H. Drummond, 1958. Reproduced by permission of the estate of the late V. H. Drummond, author, illustrator, artist and winner of the Kate Greenaway Medal for the best illustrated children's book in 1957.

gretEl KiLLeen

my Sister's a Full Stop

When tiny Eppie and tiny Zeke come **shooting** out of their mother's nose, they land **slap-bang** in the middle of a book of fairytales.

What follows is a **madcap caper**, full of laughing crocs, wicked warty witches and golden geese galore!
You'll love Zeke and Eppie's **hilariously** wacky adventures as they **fight** and **fumble** to escape the clutches of the **ZANY** fairytale world and find their way back home (but not back up Mum's nose!).

009946408X

DICK KING-SMITH

⚜ Titus ⚜
RULES OK

'Titus, my boy,' said the Queen, 'I have a funny feeling that you are going to be a very special dog.'

Titus is a young corgi puppy, growing up in Windsor Castle. There is lots he must learn (like how *not* to trip up Prince Philip!). Soon he becomes the Queen's favourite, and she even lets him sleep on her bed at night! And it is because of Titus that Her Majesty finally does something very surprising . . .

'The kind of book that would make any child want to read' *Daily Telegraph*

'Packed with lovely jokes . . . will bring joy to loyal hearts and royal ones' *Independent on Sunday*

0 552 548 375

ROBOMUM
Emily Smith

*"A robot mother?
Is that what you want?
A Robomum?"*

James's mum is a brilliant scientist, but
James wishes she was better at the ordinary
things in life. He'd really like to have a clean
PE kit, interesting food for tea and the films
that he wants on video, but Mum's got
other things on her mind. Then, in a flash
of inspiration, Mum realizes how to improve
the situation. Surely a robotic mother –
a Robomum – is just what they both need?

A highly entertaining story by an
award-winning author that will be loved
by young readers – and their mothers!

ISBN 0552 547360